A Deadly Fae Duology Novella

WINTER

Book 2.5

CASSANDRA ASTON

ISBN: 978-1-967740-07-9

Book Cover Design by: Tivuel

Illustrated Page Art by: Tivuel

Edited by: Pickles Editing & Nicole McCurdy

Content & Trigger Warnings

This book is a work of fiction. Names, characters, places, and events are products of the author's imagination. Any resemblance to actual events or persons, living or dead, is entirely coincidental. Winter is intended for mature readers and is recommended for 18+.

This book contains the following content that some readers may find difficult:

Death & Loss: Death of major characters, including a main character. Maternal death in childbirth. Implied mass death and genocide. Grief and loss throughout.

Violence: Wolf attacks and graphic animal violence. Stabbings and battle scenes. Imprisonment and captivity. Torture depicted as repeated drowning — this is a recurring, detailed scene and may be particularly distressing for sensitive readers.

Relationships & Manipulation: Political manipulation and betrayal. Parental emotional abuse and gaslighting. Power imbalance within a developing romantic relationship. Abandonment.

Other: Pregnancy and childbirth. Explicit sexual content. Morally complex characters making dark choices.

Please use caution when reading.

CONTENTS

For the ones who believe love is worth any price.
I'm so sorry.

PROLOGUE

Jack

The fire cracked softly beside me.

I hadn't meant to stop here.

I'd been pacing the tower, skimming passage after passage, chasing half-answers and loose threads until the words began to blur together. Centuries of recent history. Wars. Treaties. Names that repeated like echoes.

None of it told me who I was.

None of it told me *what* I was.

The Book of Winter rested on the small table near the hearth, its pale cover catching the firelight.

I stared at it.

If the answers existed, they wouldn't be in the last few hundred years. They would be buried deep.

At the beginning.

A knot formed in my chest. Did I really have to go all the way back?

I crossed the room and picked up the book.

The cover was bone white and smooth, not leather or anything I recognized. A constellation was etched into its surface, one I didn't know, though I'd memorized it since finding the book. Faint ornate letters curled across it in a script that matched the design of my mother's name inked on my back.

I opened it.

The poem greeted me like it always did.

Three shaped the world and cursed it with lies.
They named it their penance and looked to the skies.
Tread carefully. The stars always exact a price.

I let out a slow breath. I'd read it more times than I could count. It never changed. I still didn't understand it.

"Sav?" I called quietly.

Footsteps approached.

She appeared in the doorway, hair loose, eyes tired, wrapped in one of my spare shirts. The sight of her steadied something inside me.

I tipped the book toward her. "Will you look at it? Maybe I'm missing something obvious."

She moved closer, leaning over my shoulder. Her lips moved silently as she read. After a moment she said, "It's about the stars."

I nodded. "Yeah."

She hesitated. "Everyone in Faerie knows bargains feed them. That giving something up strengthens their influence. It's... old knowledge. Basic, almost."

My fingers tightened faintly around the book. "And the Three?" I asked gently.

Her brow furrowed. "The creators. Some believe there used to be three, not just Gaia and Luna. That they had a third sibling."

"*Believe*," I repeated.

She met my eyes. "It's just a legend."

I tried to accept what she said. To ignore the way my heart banged against my ribcage every time I repeated the words. But something about the poem shook me. Demanded I listen. And if the poem were true... Then whatever followed was too.

I'd already found one truth buried in Winter's oldest records.

Not tonight. Earlier. In a passage so fragmented it had taken me days to piece together. Mab had never been unkillable. She'd been long-lived. Gifted extended years by the Creator in exchange for two *options*. My mind circled the idea a dozen times but I couldn't make sense of it.

Still, what really mattered was that the world had been taught she was immortal because she wanted it that way. Because no one would dare challenge someone they believed unkillable.

My jaw tightened.

Sav believed Mab had given her immortality to Aconite. Most of Faerie did.

But Winter's records told a quieter, uglier story. Mab had always been killable. She'd just made sure no one knew it. I turned the page.

And Mab's words waited for me.

CHAPTER 1

Firethorn

Faerie isn't my home. The thought seared through me, hot as the fire in my veins.

The palace rose from the mountainside in sheets of ice and pale stone, its towers carved into the cliff as if the land itself had been split open to make room for us. Frost clung to every surface, and the air carried the sharp, clean bite of cold that never quite softened, no matter how long we dwelled here.

For fifty years, this had been temporary. That was what my mother had always said. We were guests here. Wayfarers between worlds. A place to rest while she searched for a realm worthy of our kind.

I had believed her.

Now she stood at the edge of the high terrace, her cloak rippling in the biting wind, the last light of a dying sun framing her in its incandescent glow. The air around her shimmered faintly, as if the world itself hesitated to let her go.

"Care for what we have claimed," Mab said, her voice steady. She did not turn to look at me. "Hold our kingdom in my absence, my son. When I return, we will remake it."

Our kingdom.

The words settled over me like ice on scorched skin.

I opened my mouth to ask what that meant. To ask when she would return. To ask why, after fifty years of calling this place a momentary reprieve, she now planned to relocate our folk to Faerie permanently.

But my mother didn't share her truths with me.

She lifted one hand to the wind and murmured something too soft for me to hear. The air tightened around her, then released, and she was simply gone. Beyond this world.

Faerie had never welcomed us.

And now she had left me here to rule it in her absence.

Winter stretched out below the palace in quiet submission, forests heavy with snow, hills and valleys white in every direction. Faerie breathed around me, ancient and patient, and for the first time since we arrived, I had the unsettling sense that it was watching to see what I would do next.

My gaze drifted, unbidden, toward the jagged peaks to the north. Somewhere beyond them lay the lands of this realm's creator. Somewhere beyond them walked the father I'd only met once.

And somewhere within Faerie itself lived my sister. Aconite.

The name surfaced, and I squeezed my fists at my sides. I remembered her only in fragments: white hair coiled around her head, tiny fingers gripping mine with too much strength for such a small thing.

She had been given to Gaia fifty years ago. A gift, my mother had said. A necessity.

I had been old enough to understand what that meant, even if I had never been allowed to say it aloud. Someone with my power could not be permitted to live in Gaia's world without assurance. A guarantee.

The guilt of that sacrifice had settled into me over time, becoming something dull and constant. But with Mab gone, the weight of it shifted, sharp again, newly unbearable.

If there had ever been a moment to find my sister, it was now. I would find Gaia and I would demand to see Aconite.

I turned from the terrace and descended through the palace halls. The palace accepted my passage without protest, its magic responding to me as it always had.

Outside the palace, my mother's magic loosened its grip.

I followed no road or carved path, striking out over snow-covered loams. The low fae didn't bow for me the way they bowed to my mother. They kept working. Bending branches into arches, carving new halls into the mountain, building a kingdom that would be my forever home.

The forest thickened as I moved south, the cold giving way to damp earth and moss slick beneath my boots. The trees were older here, their roots twisting through the soil like veins, their branches heavy with a watchfulness that made my skin prickle.

I felt it then.

A pressure. A line crossed.

A winged creature took flight and golden leaves scattered in every direction, raining around me to paint the forest floor in reds and ambers.

I slowed, every instinct sharpening.

I was not in Winter now. My mother's protection no longer wrapped around me this far from the castle.

I took another step forward, and the forest went silent.

The hairs on the back of my neck rose.

I was no longer alone.

CHAPTER 2

Firethorn

The pressure I'd felt a moment before snapped and the ground heaved beneath my feet. Stone split the soil with a grinding roar as something massive pulled itself free, shale and moss sloughing from its shoulders as it rose.

A rock troll.

It towered over me, its body half-mountain, half-moss, eyes glowing faintly from deep-set hollows as it bellowed and charged. Its magic was old and blunt, calling jagged shards of stone up from the earth in rapid succession.

I could bargain.

I could retreat.

Or I could burn my way through.

Rock trolls lived deep beneath our mountain caves. They feared flame, but it did not kill them.

Heat surged through my veins, molten and alive, pouring out of me in a wave that scorched the air. The earth beneath the troll began to glow, cracks spiderwebbing outward as my power pressed down.

The forest recoiled. Trees groaned, leaves shriveling as the magic lashed outward beyond the creature I meant to stop. I felt it then, the wild, untethered magic burning hot at my center. It had lain in wait, and the moment I was provoked, it answered.

I was burning everything.

"Enough."

The word cut through the roar of fire and stone like a blade, and something moved between us.

I checked my power hard, the fire snarling as it dragged itself back under my skin, and in that breath of hesitation, *she* appeared. She stepped between my magic and the troll, and I strained to pull the last tendrils of flame back before they could touch her.

The breath left me in a soft, stunned exhale.

Not one of the low fae or animals of the forest.

She looked... like me.

Deep amaranthine curls spilled over her shoulders, pointed ears cutting through the dark like a blade. A simple tunic was belted at her waist, and she held herself as if the forest would bend to accommodate her. Long limbs stretched toward the ground, sure-footed and balanced, bare feet planted on mossy loam.

My gaze caught on the curve of her hips, the line of a collarbone, before snapping back to her face as my mind finally caught up with what my eyes were seeing.

For a heartbeat, my thoughts stalled. I had only ever seen two beings like me.

My mother and sister.

A sudden wall of wind tore through the clearing, snapping branches and knocking me another step back. The last of my heat bled into the ground, leaving the air ringing with silence.

She turned her head slowly, surveying the damage, before her gaze cut back to me, eyes locking on mine, sharp and furious.

"Are you trying to decimate this forest and its folk, or are you simply careless?"

I stared at her, words lodged uselessly in my throat.

She smelled like warm air over water lilies. Sunlight trapped on a breeze. Fresh. Alive. Nothing like Winter.

Behind her, the troll struggled to stand.

She didn't look back as she lifted one hand and made a sound low in her throat, part command, part warning, and the troll stopped. Its massive form shuddered, stone grinding against stone, before it backed away, sinking into the earth as if the forest itself were swallowing it whole.

The ground stilled.

Only then did she face me fully, and my heart beat hard from the weight of her gaze.

"You don't belong here." She crossed her arms over her chest.

"I'm as free to roam in Faerie as any other creature."

A corner of her mouth twitched. Not a smile. Something sharper. "That is not what this place is called."

I opened my mouth to argue, then stopped.

"What are you?" I asked instead.

Her gaze swept over me, unflinching. "Someone who cleans up messes left by children with too much magic in their veins."

Heat flared in my chest, reflexive and unwanted. "You stood between me and a threat."

"You would have burned this forest to the ground," she snapped. "If you had finished what you started, there would be nothing left but scorched stone."

I stiffened, looking at the blackened earth around us, the singed leaves curling at the edges, and for the first time wondered if Oceanus's distaste for cold wasn't the only reason we had been forced to live in Winter.

"You think strength gives you the right to burn whatever you please," she continued. "It doesn't."

"I had it under control."

She tilted her head. "You didn't."

I thought of Aconite then. Of white hair and small hands. Of the promise my mother had made to Gaia.

The thought cooled something reckless inside me.

"I wasn't trying to hurt anyone," I said softly.

Her lips flattened. "Intent does not spare the land."

She stepped back, already retreating, already done with me. "Leave," she said. "And don't come this far south again."

"No." I squared my shoulders.

She paused.

"Tell me your name," I said. "Where you live. So I may find you again."

Her eyes narrowed, assessing me.

Without a word, she turned and vanished into the trees, the forest closing around her as if she had never been there.

"Wait," I started forward, but the undergrowth swallowed her footprints, and the air held no trace of her passage.

I stopped among scorched earth and curling smoke, my pulse still racing, my magic restless beneath my skin.

The female whose name I didn't know had saved this place from me. And if I proved myself a threat, it wouldn't be me who paid the price.

I turned back toward Winter, my jaw clenched hard enough to ache, but her scent hung in the air around me, and the question burned hotter than any fire I'd called.

How could there be another like me in Faerie?

CHAPTER 3

Firethorn

Winter found me again the moment I crossed the invisible line my mother had drawn. Magic slid over my shoulders like a cloak, cold and familiar, tightening until my chest ached. The air grew still. The wind lost its teeth. Even the snow seemed to fall in tidy spirals instead of being flung wherever it pleased.

In the forest, everything had breathed. Here, everything was leashed.

Shadows appeared on the horizon.

They emerged from the trees in a silent line, pale as bone white against the snow, their bodies too smooth to be natural, no unevenness in their gait.

Mother's wolves.

The leader's eyes caught mine, glittering emerald, like my mother's. They didn't smell like beasts. They smelled like Winter. Like the palace stone and the faint tang that clung to everything my mother shaped.

I walked, and they fell in beside me.

I could burn them. The thought came as quickly as it always did, bright and vicious, and I swallowed it down. The wolves had done nothing wrong. They were what she made them to be.

Ahead, the palace rose from the mountainside, ice and pale stone fused so seamlessly into the cliff that it sometimes looked as if the mountain itself had grown towers. Fifty years ago, it had been little more than a sheer cliff face. A refuge.

Now it was a statement.

As I passed beneath the first arch, Winter's magic pressed in, wrapping around my bones with familiar insistence. The palace accepted me, its wards recognizing my blood. The wolves peeled away and vanished into the snow.

Inside, the air smelled faintly of smoke and stone dust.

Beyond the great hall lay corridors I knew well. Armories, war rooms, and the cold, silent library where I had passed countless hours among my mother's books and records. I followed it.

The great hall hummed with labor. Low fae moved through the space in coordinated swarms, hauling baskets of rock and ice, dragging timber that should have weighed more than their slight bodies could bear. They did not complain.

I found the source of the smoke at the mouth of a new passage cut into the mountain.

The tunnel yawned beyond the hall, raw stone carved wide enough for a cart. Torches lined the walls, their light catching flecks in the rock. Some were dull. Some flashed when the flame struck them at the right angle.

Gems.

The low fae were mining. Supports had been driven into the stone. Crews chipped glittering fragments from the walls and gathered them into baskets. Others hauled the baskets deeper into the palace.

Suddenly, my mother's plan was clear. She had carved more than a refuge from this frozen place. She had found resources to be hoarded.

A low fae glanced up at me and froze. Then he bowed hastily, forehead nearly touching the ground.

"You don't need to do that," I said.

He didn't rise.

A memory surfaced. My mother on this floor, long ago, when the palace was still more cave than castle. A troll had brought her gems larger than her fist. An offering.

Her mouth curved faintly. Then she spoke a name. Not a name like mine. Something older. The troll went still, every joint locking in place, his massive form shuddering once before he began to back away, sinking into the earth as if the rocks were swallowing him whole.

"They are wild," she had explained after he was gone. "They do not understand order. So I guide them."

Guide. As if she had not reached inside him and pulled out his will.

Heat stirred under my skin. I forced my fingers to relax.

The low fae worker backed away, basket clutched to his chest. I wanted to stop him, to explain that my anger wasn't for him, but for his treatment, but I held my tongue. Nothing I said would convince them not to fear me. I had tried time and again.

Down the hall, a boy stumbled under the weight of another basket. His knees buckled.

I stepped forward, but a wolf slipped from the shadows. Its teeth caught the handle and lifted the load with ease. The boy stared, wide-eyed, then hurried on without a word.

Protection, my mother would call it. But her wolves were nothing but a reminder that she was always watching.

I turned away from the tunnel and marched back into the great hall. The low fae kept working. The wolves paced the edges like pale ghosts.

A small fawn stood near one of the pillars, watching me approach and extended a pouch when I reached her.

"For what?" I asked.

"Don't use your fire," she said quietly. "Please."

I ground my teeth and took the pouch. Word had traveled of my fiery outburst in the forest and like the others, nothing I said would convince this low fae I hadn't meant anyone harm. It smelled of sweet herbs, fresh and green, unmistakably gathered from beyond Winter's border. A reminder of what I could destroy.

"I won't," I said, offering what little I could.

She nodded once and disappeared into the shadows.

I stood, the pouch clenched in my hand, the mountain's cold settling deep in my bones, and thought of the forest south of here. Of how the land had pushed back against my fire. Of the way the high fae female had stopped the troll without forcing it.

She had not needed magic. She belonged.

I turned toward the palace doors.

CHAPTER 4

Lorelai

The sea knew before I did.

It always did.

The water pulled tight along the cliffs, restless and uneasy, its rhythm shifting beneath my feet as if something deep below had turned in its sleep. I stood at the edge of the stone overlook, wind tugging at my hair, and listened as the tide whispered warnings not yet shaped into words.

He had crossed the boundary. *Firethorn.*

I felt him the way one feels a coming storm before the clouds gather. A heat where there should have been none.

I exhaled slowly, bracing my palms against the cold stone. The sea stirred in answer, not in fear, but in recognition.

Behind me, the air shifted.

"You felt it," my father said.

I didn't turn. "The mountain woke."

"The mountain answered," he corrected gently.

That made my back stiffen.

He joined me at the cliff's edge, his presence heavy but familiar. The Sea King had not changed over the centuries. His hair still fell in turquoise sheets down his back, and his eyes still held the deep, unlit blue of the trenches where light never dared to reach. Power clung to him, drenching the air and rocks around him.

"I don't trust him to allow Luna's passage," I said.

Oceanus tilted his head, unbothered. "Luna will do as she's always done. Do you believe he could stop a deity even if he wanted to?"

"He is Mab's offspring, and she has already broken her promise."

"*She* has not," my father replied. "She is not in our realm at present."

I turned then, anger sparking hot in my chest. "Is your bargain with her nullified when she leaves the planet? He crossed the boundary. He burned the wilds."

My temper slipped, and the sea answered. Waves drew back before crashing against the rocks with sudden violence. I forced myself to breathe, keeping my power leashed.

"Her bargain ensures she will keep his magic contained, not *him*."

"He is not contained," I said. "You felt it. His power is untrained. Untempered. He could tear this realm apart."

My father studied the horizon. "Or he could become something else."

The sound that left me held no warmth. "You sound like your advisors."

Oceanus pressed his lips together, gaze returning to the waves already surging.

"We must prepare for Luna's crossing," I said, bitterness bleeding into my voice. "Holding the sea in her absence will take all I have. If he chooses now to make a move, Peloria will not be safe."

Luna had begun her descent. In a matter of days, the sea would rage and controlling it would be on my shoulders. I had seen my father hold the sea without her more than once, but it had never been my responsibility.

When he said nothing, I continued: "You should have destroyed him when you had the chance."

"He is not our enemy."

"He is a weapon."

The sea surged closer. My father's voice remained calm. "You will go to him."

The words struck like a slap.

"No."

"You will," he said quietly. "You will speak to him. You will steady him."

My chin lifted sharply. "You want me to hold a firestorm by the throat?"

"I want you to protect Peloria."

"By deceiving him."

"By guiding him."

I shook my head. "He is not some lost child. He is a force. And you want to hand him to me like a burden I should be grateful to bear?"

"I want you to keep him from becoming what he could be."

Silence stretched between us.

"And when he realizes what I am?" I asked quietly.

My father's gaze softened just enough to hurt. "By then, it will not matter."

Cold slid through me.

"You want me to make him trust me."

"Yes."

I turned away before he could see the fury rising in my eyes. "You're asking me to put myself within reach."

"I'm asking you to get close enough to stop him should the need arise."

The sea roared below us, wild and restless. I had days to accomplish his impossible task. Days before I would be too drained to take him by force.

I closed my eyes.

"Is this a command?" I asked.

"Yes."

CHAPTER 5

Firethorn

I returned to the southern forest with my pride raw. The first time I crossed that line, I had scorched the land with no concern for the damage I could cause.

Now I moved with care.

I kept my power leashed so tightly it ached. The cold of Winter faded behind me, not all at once, but in loosening tendrils. Snow scattered and dissolved, stone softening into damp earth. Pines gave way to older trees, their roots tangled deep as if they had been holding this ground together long before my mother ever carved her castle into this world.

Every step south felt like trespass.

Not because the land resisted me. Because it remembered.

The forest stretched wide, mushrooms and strange flora dotted its carpet. Branches snagged at my sleeves. I reached a stream and bent to drink, cupping my hands. The water was tepid and fresh, nothing like the snow I melted in the mountains.

My mother was terrified of granting the Sea King access. In Winter no streams flowed, and the ocean lay days from our eastern border. It was not that he could not travel over land. He could. But far from his source of magic, he weakened.

A splash sounded.

I looked up.

Around me, the forest remained silent, its folk hidden. Whoever had made the sound was gone.

Not Aconite. Unless she, too, chose to hide rather than face the one who burned the world that offered us refuge.

My hands curled at my sides, nails biting into my palms. The guilt never left. It shifted, settling deeper when ignored, sharpening when remembered.

If I found Gaia, I would demand my sister back. If I found Aconite, I didn't know what I would do. I had scoured my mother's books and notes for any mention of Gaia. They yielded nothing. I didn't know whether Gaia had poisoned my sister's mind. Whether she would see kin or betrayal.

Fleetingly, I wished I had brought my charcoal and paper. I could have sketched the world around me. Cataloged all I saw as mother did.

The wind changed. Warmth threaded through it, gentle as breath against skin. It drifted through the trees from farther south, carrying the faint scent of crushed leaves and something sweet, like flowers warmed by the sun.

I stopped.

My heart kicked once, stupidly hopeful.

Her?

The high fae female with amaranthine hair and eyes like a blade's edge. The one who had stepped between my fire and the forest without fear. The one who had told me strength did not grant permission.

I told myself I returned for Aconite, and it was true. But there was another pull that had nothing to do with guilt.

I followed the warmth.

The trees thinned into a hollow where the earth dipped low, cradling a small pool fed by a spring slipping from the rocks. At the far side stood a doe. At first glance, it looked ordinary. Slender legs. Soft brown coat. Wide ears angled toward me. Then the light struck its antlers.

They were not antlers but branching light, delicate and luminous. The doe lifted her head, and intelligence met my gaze.

Recognition stirred under my skin as the doe stepped forward. Where her hoof touched the moss-covered floor, pale light rippled outward in a slow ring.

My throat tightened. "Hello. Can you..."

The words dissolved when a voice sounded in my mind. *Firethorn.* My name landed with unsettling familiarity.

"Who are you?" I whispered.

The light shifted, and she became fae-shaped, luminous curls falling around her shoulders, hooved feet planted in moss.

Not fae.

Something else.

"I'm Luna," she said aloud, her voice vibrating through the air like a chord.

My pulse thundered. "You are one of the creators of this realm."

"And you are not one of my creations," she replied.

I forced myself to breathe. "Why are you here?"

"To return where I belong."

"Where you belong?"

"My realm. So that I may restore what I have spent."

My gaze lifted instinctively toward the canopy. "Who will light the world by night?" I asked.

"The stars wait a century for their moment," Luna said, following my gaze up. "But they are not kind. Be wary of their eyes."

The warning settled deep.

We walked in silence. Her power wrapped around me like silk, soft but unyielding. Creatures emerged as we passed, paying me no mind.

I stole a glance at Luna, trying and failing to find similarities between her and my father. They were both deities—were they related in the way folk were? Or did that word mean something different for beings like them? Would she know where I could find him?

A winged creature landed nearby and I wondered what it was called.

"Harpy," Luna said.

I startled. "You can read my mind."

"Yes." She touched the creature's wing, and an old wound sealed itself, soft light streaming along the tear. "You want to know about your father."

Heat crept up my neck.

"We are not bound by blood as mortals are," she said. "My siblings and I were shaped from a single energy source, but we do not share lineage."

She resumed walking.

"Curiosity is not a failing," she added. "But seeking what you cannot change will only teach you how to suffer."

The harpy launched skyward and vanished.

"Beyond the mountain," Luna said, "our kind find respite from this realm's demands."

Our kind. My heart lurched. Did that mean she considered me one of them?

Ignoring my thoughts, she went on. "Your father grew weary. He searched for others like us. None were found."

I considered her words. "Is that why he made more like you?"

She rested a hand on my shoulder. Steam rose where her magic met mine. "Like *us*, Nephew."

Thoughts fought for dominance. Did they seek a continuation of their line? Why had he created me if he chose not to seek me out? Was he truly lonely or only seeking a continuation of his line? In the end, I only asked: "Why?"

She resumed walking. "He hoped to set his burdens down."

The meaning formed slowly. "So he made someone who could take up his work. Heirs."

"Options," Luna corrected. The word landed wrong. Not family, but a term you used for a tool you might discard. "You are not the only ones."

The pieces aligned with sudden clarity.

"The Sea King," I said. "With that much power... Oceanus is my half brother."

Luna stopped, turning to face me.

"No," she said quietly. "Oceanus is mine."

CHAPTER 6

Firethorn

Luna didn't look at me as her voice slid into my mind. *The sea is ruled by my son.*

I walked faster, rushing to keep pace. "So he'll take your place? In the sky?"

Luna's laugh was quiet. "No."

Her eyes cut to me, no longer brown but an alien silver.

"I have other plans for Oceanus."

My boots crunched on snow and I shivered, glancing to Luna, still bare from head to hoof, but she did not appear affected by the elements.

As we crested a hill, the castle came into view. Luna stopped, turning to me. "This is where I leave you, Nephew."

Panic seized me, a dozen questions tripping over one another. Before I could form any of them, she looked up at the darkening sky. My gaze followed hers to what would be a moonless night without her.

Her eyes met mine as she looked down. "Be wary of those glittering daggers in the stygian sky. In my absence they will attempt to cajole. Do not be fooled by them. They seek what they can never have."

I frowned, but before I could ask more, the air shimmered and she was gone.

I stood for a moment, frosty air clouding my vision. Then I spun away from the castle and my mother's chains.

Deep within the wilds, animals moved freely now. Had Luna changed something, or did they recognize me for what I truly was?

Now I knew how vitally important it was to find my sister and tell her all I'd learned.

I moved quickly, not wasting time covering my tracks. This realm was large and the last time I'd seen my sister, nearly fifty years ago, Gaia met us at the border of Winter, disappearing into the forest without a backward glance. They could be anywhere. How did one find a forest goddess?

Hissing erupted at my feet and I glanced down. Tiny flora with scaled heads spat fire and made tiny roaring noises. I bent, inspecting them closely. Their golden flames sparked harmlessly off my skin and I grinned. Many things could harm me in Faerie, but fire wasn't one of them.

"Hello," I said, extending a hand toward the nearest creature. It snapped viciously but was restrained by the stalk tethering it to the ground. "Don't be afraid. I won't harm you. I'm looking for a goddess."

The tiny flowers stopped their hissing and, as one, faced me.

"I believe I'm searching for your creator."

"Mother," one said in a rasping voice.

I nodded. It seemed right that the creatures would see her as their mother.

They whispered, several spreading scaled petals wide to obscure their conversation from view. Even soft-spoken, I heard everything. They debated whether I could be trusted. Some argued in favor of a creature with fire magic like their own. Others reminded the group I was not born of this world, an outsider who might have malicious intentions.

In the end, they chose to trust me.

"She rests beyond the sparkling falls, past the white wall and underneath the crimson canopy," the floral creature that had first addressed me said.

I puzzled over their words. I had never ventured so far beyond Winter, and although I understood some of what they described, I had no idea what direction to head.

"Will you show me?" I asked.

The nearest bloom tugged its roots from the earth and marched toward my boot. It pointed a petal at my hand. I held my palm flat as it climbed on top, and I lifted it, getting a closer look. Its shape was vaguely floral, but its scaly petals shimmered in iridescent gold and blue. Tiny nostrils puffed smoke.

It crossed two petals over its dusky stalk and narrowed its black eyes at me. "If we guide you, what do we get?"

I slid a hand into my pocket and pulled out one of the gemstones from my mother's mines, then hesitated. Would a field of flowers value a stone? I tucked it away again. "A promise," I said. It arched a tiny eyebrow. "If you set me on my path, I'll owe you something later. I'll decide what that thing is."

The flower's brow pinched, but it did not consult the others before dipping its chin. "We accept. But should you perish, we want repayment from your kin. Put me down and we'll show you."

I grinned and set the creature on the moss.

Before my eyes, the creature twisted until the underside of its petals showed. They were nearly white against the forest floor. A line formed as each flower followed suit. Small arrows appeared, pointing south.

A grin split my lips.

"Wonderful. What can I call you?"

One of the flowers tipped its head toward me. "We are SnapDragons."

I nodded, smiling to myself as I followed the series of white dashes with the occasional arrow directing me south, until I was beside a stream and the SnapDragons led the way.

CHAPTER 7

Lorelai

The ocean shifted beneath the cliffs, drawing back in a slow, uneasy breath that made the rocks tremble under my feet. The tide did not retreat as it should. It hesitated, uncertain, then surged forward again, as if trying to find the rhythm it had lost.

I stood on the overlook above the water, palms braced on stone, and listened.

The sea was restless.

A thin line of foam broke against the rocks below, then vanished. In the distance, the surface darkened where a storm should not have been forming. Lightning flickered within the clouds like a warning.

I lifted my gaze. The sky was scattered with stars, sharp and cold.

No moon.

The emptiness where it should have been made my ribs ache. It was one thing to know Luna could leave and my father would bear the brunt of the consequence. It was another to see the sky stripped bare and realize how much the world relied on her presence.

Behind me, the air shifted.

"It has begun," Oceanus said.

I didn't turn. "The tides can't find her."

Oceanus stepped beside me, his gaze fixed on the horizon. In his eyes, I saw the endless certainty of someone who had held this world together longer than most creatures had existed.

"She will return," he said.

"The ocean was not so unsettled the last time she left."

"You will learn to control it."

Waves surged below, slamming against the rocks harder than they should have. Spray leapt up the cliff face.

My jaw tightened. "How long will she be gone?"

"A handful of nights," Oceanus said. "And in the meantime, you will hold it."

I exhaled slowly, emptying my lungs until my chest felt hollow. I had been preparing for this for years.

I closed my eyes and let my awareness sink into the currents, the deep channels, the vast pressure holding the world's water in place.

It was alive. Restless. Ancient.

I pressed my palm to the stone and let my power slip beneath the waves, shaping rather than seizing. "Luna guide me," I whispered.

The water answered.

The violent surge beneath the cliffs slowed. The tide hesitated, then settled into a fragile rhythm. Storm clouds in the distance stalled, their lightning fading.

The pressure was immediate. My shoulders tensed as the sea pushed back, vast and unrelenting. My magic burned. It was not limitless, but it was deep enough to draw from, if I was careful.

"Hold it," Oceanus said calmly.

I adjusted, letting the rhythm move through me instead of against me. The water followed. The tightness in my center eased, though the drain did not.

"There," Oceanus said at last. "It will grow easier with time."

I nodded, fingers trembling as I steadied myself. The sea remained restless beneath me, its rhythm imperfect, reaching for Luna's pull and finding only absence.

Then heat threaded through the water, subtle but unmistakable.

I gasped.

"You felt him," Oceanus said.

"He's near."

"He crossed the boundary again."

"He's moving south."

The ocean stirred, like a body shifting in uneasy sleep. My magic tightened reflexively, maintaining the fragile balance.

"You must have it under control before you seek him out," Oceanus said.

I turned sharply. "Surely this can wait until Luna returns."

His lips flattened into a line. For a moment, there was only heavy silence between us. Then he said, "We do not have time."

I searched his cold, hard face for any sign there was a father beneath the king's command.

"I can't," I finally said.

"You must," Oceanus replied. "Our future is at stake."

My stomach twisted.

"Mab is off world," I murmured.

Oceanus's eyes snapped to mine. "She is no threat to us. Firethorn threatens your legacy."

"He holds no claim over the sea."

"The claim he holds is far greater than that," Oceanus said quietly. "He could destroy this world. If his father chose to pass on his legacy. He is not of this world. Do you trust that he would protect it as we would?"

The ocean shivered beneath the cliffs, its rhythm faltering. I forced my focus back into it, holding the pattern steady.

I could hold it. I had to.

But every moment proved what Oceanus had not yet said aloud.

One day, he would not be here to catch me if I slipped.

I looked inland, toward the unseen boundary where Winter ended and the wilds began.

CHAPTER 8

Firethorn

The SnapDragons' trail twisted and wound, following the stream for long stretches before dipping into the forest to wind between massive, ancient tree trunks. There must have been hundreds of thousands of the flora, their guidance carried along some unseen network.

The air grew warmer and damper as I followed the path. The canopy thickened and insects buzzed against my ears. Somewhere ahead, water burbled over stone.

I followed the sound, boots sinking into soft earth, senses stretched taut, listening for any shift in the forest's breath.

Luna's words circled my thoughts. My mother had brought us here pregnant with my sister, calling this realm a stopping point, not our destination, yet this was my father's world.

What had changed? Why did she want to stay now?

The SnapDragon trail ended abruptly, halting my thoughts.

I turned in a slow circle. Only the path behind me remained, the flowers stretching their petals wide toward the fading light, no longer guiding my way.

The forest offered no sign of Gaia or my sister. Instead, a familiar warmth lingered on the air.

Warm air over water lilies. Sunlight trapped on a breeze.

I stilled.

It was the scent of the high fae female who had stepped between my fire and the forest.

Following it, I moved through thinning trees that broke open onto a meadow. At its center, a shallow pool lay cradled in stone.

Plum-dark curls caught my eye at once. At the water's edge, she stood with her back to me, hands braced on a rock, head bowed. A sharp breath left her. The water rippled outward in a perfect circle.

At the tree line, I stopped.

She whispered something too low for me to catch. The water stilled, then moved with her, rising and falling in a controlled rhythm. Her shoulders shook once, and the pool shuddered.

I stepped forward.

A twig snapped.

Her head lifted and she turned.

Sea glass eyes that had haunted me since our first encounter, locked on mine, bright at the edges, darker at the center. Dark circles rimmed them.

"Firethorn," she said.

She knew my name. I wished more than anything to know hers. Would she give it?

I took a careful step closer. She tensed but did not retreat. "I had hoped I'd see you again."

A faint, almost amused sound escaped her before tightening into something guarded. "You're looking for Gaia," she said.

"Yes. Do you know where she is?"

"I know a great many things."

Her answer sounded like my mother. My jaw clenched.

"Will you tell me what to call you?"

She hesitated.

"Lorelai."

The name lodged beneath my ribs, unwelcome and impossible to ignore.

"Why are you here?" I asked.

"Because you're dangerous."

"You came for me." A grin tugged at my mouth as my shoulders relaxed.

"I came to make sure you didn't destroy any more forests."

I studied her more closely. A tremor in her hands. The faint sheen of sweat at her hairline.

"Are you unwell?"

"No."

The stream rippled beside her. She blinked, gaze unfocused for a heartbeat.

"Let me help you," I said.

"I don't need your help."

She turned sharply toward the trees.

"Wait."

She stopped but did not face me.

"Don't go. Please." The words escaped my mouth in a plea. "I have no one."

She turned back, pale and swaying.

I moved as her knees buckled, catching her before she fell. "The pond," she gasped.

"What?" I wrapped an arm around her. "You're freezing. Let me build a fire."

"No," she said. "Water. Help me into the water."

I hesitated only a moment before lifting her. She protested weakly, then went limp against me as I carried her to the pool and lowered her beside it.

She slid forward, dipping her feet in. Color returned to her cheeks. She exhaled, the tension easing from her face.

I backed away, breath unsteady. "You're a sea creature."

She looked up, eyes sharp again. "I never said I wasn't."

"Were you sent by the Sea King to kill me?"

She let out a shaky laugh. "Your mother's bargain ensures that could never happen."

Bargain? I studied her, unsettled. She did not look like any of the sea folk from my mother's drawings. They were often scaled, with thin slits at their throats. Mab had written that shifters could often breathe on land, but none of her descriptions had ever painted them as looking so... fae.

"Why were you looking for me?"

"To ensure you did not destroy more of my world."

I stiffened. "I have as much right to it as anyone."

The water beneath her rippled, then calmed as she breathed out, but she said nothing.

"Will you tell me where to find Gaia?" I asked.

The moment her foot left the water, her skin cooled, her eyes rolling back in her head.

I caught her as she collapsed. Her body was too cold.

Supporting her head, I laid her in the moss, watching her chest rise and fall. A quiet unease crept through me. Whatever this was, she needed rest. I searched the forest for any signs of danger. I shouldn't leave her here defenseless, even if she was a sea fae.

I looked down again, cataloging her slender nose, delicate features, and smooth skin.

Her lashes fluttered, then stilled.

The air shifted.

My breath caught as her form blurred. Hair thickened and darkened. Violet scales rippled down her arms. Lines etched themselves along her throat.

A kelpie.

I swallowed hard, one knee pressed into the moss. I should go while she was unconscious. I'd been lucky I survived our first encounter. I searched her face again. And yet... Leaving her, regardless of the strain between our courts, felt wrong.

I draped my cloak over her shoulders, covering what I could. Heat gathered instinctively in my palms but I forced it down. Fire would not help her.

I cupped water from the pool and brushed it against her lips.

She swallowed reflexively, eyelids fluttering again.

Good.

I repeated it, slower this time, then sat back and waited.

Time passed. Light dimmed as clouds drifted overhead.

Her breathing steadied.

The shimmer faded. Scales smoothed into skin. Her hair softened, lightening as it curled around her face.

When her eyes finally opened, confusion clouded them.

Then she realized where she was.

She tried to sit up and winced.

"Don't. You'll fall," I said. "You passed out."

She pushed herself up more slowly, gaze darting to the cloak, then back to me.

"Neat trick," I said.

Her brow furrowed. "What?"

"Making yourself look like my kind."

Recognition crossed her face, followed by mortification. "I didn't do it on purpose."

"You mean you can't control it."

She looked away. "All of my kind have a gift. Mine shows you what you most want to see."

I went still.

"I don't know what I look like," she said quietly. "Mirrors only show me what I want to see."

I knew that feeling. Not the magic, but the weight of never being seen past what others had already decided you were.

"I should go," she said, pushing herself upright.

"You won't make it back to the ocean alone."

"I must."

I stood and offered my hand.

She flinched back as if *she* were afraid of *me*.

"Trust me?"

She stared at me. Eyes piercing through to my very soul. I stilled as she came to some decision and accepted my hand.

Pulling her up, I steadied her as she swayed. "May I carry you?"

Her hesitation was shorter this time and my chest buzzed when she nodded.

I lifted her into my arms, holding her close as her breathing evened out.

CHAPTER 9

Lorelai

His arms were warm and steady, and though letting him carry me was a terrible idea, not all of my weakness had been feigned. Being this far from the water took more from me than I liked to admit.

The moment he found me, I had planned a careful ruse. The oldest story. A helpless girl in need of saving. Instead, exhaustion had stripped the plan bare.

I wondered what he had seen when I lost consciousness. What version of me the magic had chosen. I had not seen my true face since I was twelve, and even that memory had blurred with time.

I had stopped looking in mirrors long ago.

"Behind the rock wall, you'll need to turn south," I said, watching the set of his jaw.

He glanced down at me, and I noticed his eyes were green. Bright and warm, nothing like the cold creature my father had described.

His lips tipped in a faint, absurd grin. He thought himself a hero. I would use that.

"I'm looking for my sister," he said.

"Aconite?"

His muscles went taut. "How do you know her name?"

I lifted a hand and rested it against his chest. His heart jumped beneath my palm.

"Everyone knows of her."

His grip loosened.

"If you want, I can take you to her."

Warmth lit his eyes, hope too quick and too raw. Reuniting them might be a mistake. Two forces like that in one place could unmake the balance we relied upon.

I told myself it was strategy. That the hope in his eyes was simply a weakness to be mapped and used. That was all this was.

I almost believed it.

He nodded.

We traveled until the sun slipped from the sky. Without Luna's light, the forest closed in around us. Firethorn stumbled over roots and branches, breath sharp with exertion.

"We need to stop," he said, setting me gently against a tree. He draped his cloak over my shoulders. "I'll make a small fire."

He moved away, cursing softly as he gathered leaves and bark. Sparks leapt from his fingers and flame bloomed in his palms.

I studied it, noting the perfect circle. Controlled. Ruled.

"When you've recovered," he asked quietly, "will you tell me about her?"

"Yes," I said.

CHAPTER 10

Firethorn

In sleep, Lorelai's eyes twitched, her fingers curling into fists before relaxing again. Whatever haunted her dreams followed her even now. I found myself wanting to know what those demons were, to chase them away.

I studied her in the firelight.

Was she telling the truth? Did I truly see what I most wanted to see when I looked at her? Another high fae. Someone like me. The thought tightened something in my chest before I could stop it.

Now that I knew it was a facade, I noticed the inconsistencies the magic couldn't hide. A faint shimmer to her hair. Iridescence along her throat where my cloak slipped. The longer I watched, the more the illusion softened, revealing the creature beneath.

We were far from Winter now. My mother's magic no longer pressed against my skin, no longer leashed the fire in my veins. Here, among damp earth and fallen leaves, my power settled instead of straining.

The flames beside us burned low and steady, exactly where I had willed it to remain. Lorelai's breathing evened, her shoulders no longer trembling.

I leaned back against the tree and closed my eyes.

The fire hummed contentedly.

Something brushed my face.

I jolted awake, heat flaring instinctively before I forced it down. A satyr leaned back from me, golden eyes wide as she studied Lorelai.

"Prince," the low fae said.

I swallowed and glanced past her to Lorelai. She was awake now, watching with sharp focus.

"He's with me, Antemysa," Lorelai said.

The satyr's gaze flicked to the fire. "You protect the fire prince?"

"We're going to the sea," Lorelai said.

"My forest has no accord with Mab," Antemysa replied. A spear appeared in her hand, its tip pressed to my throat before I could move.

"I'm not your enemy," I said carefully.

The air thickened. Moisture gathered along my skin.

Lightning struck the earth beside us with a deafening crack. Antemysa stumbled back, eyes slitted as she turned toward Lorelai.

"Stop," I shouted. Heat burned in my veins, desperate to be unleashed, but I held it back."We'll leave," I said. "Just let us pass."

The sky darkened again, charged and waiting.

At last, Antemysa lowered her spear. "When you reach the sea," she said to Lorelai, "tell your father he owes me."

I grabbed Lorelai's hand and ran.

We didn't stop until the forest thinned into sand and black barked trees stretched into the distance.

"We can stop," Lorelai said, breathless. "We're past her lands."

I turned to her. She was pale, trembling, but standing.

"That was some gift," I said.

"And you?" she asked. "Why didn't you defend yourself?"

"And prove I'm the monster you all think I am?"

"You burned the rock troll."

"Rock trolls don't die by my fire," I said. "And you weren't pleased the last time I used my gift."

Silence stretched between us.

"Your father is the king," I said.

"Yes."

"Why didn't you tell me?"

"Would you have trusted me?"

Probably not. I let my silence answer.

"You seem well enough to continue on your own," I said. "Perhaps we should part ways."

Her face fell.

"What about your sister?" she asked quietly.

I stuffed my hands into my pockets. The realm was vast. Even retracing my steps, I had no idea where Gaia or Aconite might be. But going with her meant trusting the Sea King's daughter. Was I foolish enough to trust the daughter of the male even my mother feared?

She stepped closer, touching my arm. "You don't have to come with me," she said. "But don't walk into that forest alone."

CHAPTER 11

Lorelai

Antemysa had chosen the worst possible moment to reveal herself. Her words had cut straight through my careful pretense. The prince would not trust me now.

I would have to try a different approach.

His burning gaze met mine and I saw it. Desire. He wanted me. Or whatever I looked like to him. But would it be enough to convince him?

He searched my face for an uncomfortably long time, seeking some answer I wasn't sure I had. The storm overhead had dissipated and with it, my terror. Why had I cared so much what happened to him? Because of Mab's bargain? But the bargain didn't stipulate we keep him safe, only that no sea creature could harm him.

A week ago, I would have watched as she ended him and been glad of one less threat to our world.

"Can I trust you?"

His words made my skin prickle. It was a damn good question.

"I saved your life did I not?"

His lips tipped up and my stomach swooped. "I suppose you did."

I cleared my throat. "Good. We're nearly to the ocean. Accompany me and after, I'll help you find your sister."

His grin vanished. "I thought you knew where she was."

I frowned. "I have an idea."

His jaw flexed, his shoulders tensing.

I lifted a hand to my temple, wiping away the sweat gathering there. It was warmer here, but my body was reacting to the magic strain more than the weather.

Firethorn's posture relaxed. His brow furrowed. "I said I would take you to the ocean and I will."

I let my knees soften and swayed.

Firethorn's hand closed around my arm at once, steadying me. His grip was firm, but careful, as though he feared I might break.

"You are unwell," he said.

"A little."

We moved more slowly after that. He adjusted his pace without comment, staying close.

A sharp chitter cut through the underbrush.

Firethorn halted.

So did I.

Something flickered between the roots of a fallen tree. A spark snapped against a leaf, leaving a blackened mark on its surface.

A round of sharp, high pitched curses burst from behind the tree.

I followed Firethorn as he approached the felled trunk.

A pixie tangled in vines, one narrow wing pinned beneath a coil of barbs, snapped wildly, spitting pinpricks of fire no larger than embers.

Firethorn took a step toward her.

"Don't," I said.

He glanced back. "Does she bite?"

"Don't mistake her size for harmlessness."

Both his brows shot up. He considered my words before squaring his shoulders and turning back to the creature anyway.

I watched him, waiting for the monster he was said to be. It was one thing to face a powerful clan leader. It was another to stand before someone small, trapped, and afraid.

Firethorn lowered himself onto one knee.

The pixie shrieked and hurled a spark of glittering fire, striking him in the chest.

He didn't flinch as he lifted his hands. "I will not harm you."

The pixie shot three more tiny fireballs at him.

Firethorn moved slowly, reaching for the vines, testing their strength. A barb bit into his fingers and crimson welled on the pad of his thumb. *Crimson*, like the other land creatures in Peloria.

He ignored it, working the thorns apart strand by strand. The pixie fought her restraints, struggling against the tangle of thorns and he stilled, murmuring soothing words to the frightened creature. When she quieted, he continued.

At last, the trapped wing slipped free.

The pixie hesitated, crouched to launch herself into the sky, then gave a tiny cry when her torn wing fluttered. A sparkling tear welled and dripped down her cheek.

Firethorn tore a narrow strip from the hem of his sleeve and set it upon the earth between them.

"Wrap this around your wing until it heals."

The pixie stared at the cloth for a long moment before she darted forward, seized it, and vanished into the fallen tree.

Firethorn remained kneeling a moment longer.

Then he rose and wiped his blood streaked finger on his pantleg, meeting my eyes.

This was not what I had expected of the Prince of Winter.

We stared at one another for a long silent moment. Then, I said, "I promised I'd tell you about your sister."

"I had been called to the marsh clan," I said, not waiting for his reply. "Mudslides had torn through an entire village."

I started forward. After a moment, he followed, close enough that I could feel his presence at my side.

"I found Gaia at the edge of the flooding. The ground kept giving way beneath what remained of their homes. She was holding the land together long enough for survivors to be pulled free."

I watched the path ahead as we walked.

"Your sister was with her. Inside a collapsed structure. Carrying folk out. Healing the ones who could still be saved."

His jaw tightened.

"She moved through them without hesitation. Young. Old. Anyone she could reach." Silence stretched between us. "By the time it was over, she could barely stand," I said. "But she stayed. Until the last survivor was clear."

"The land folk speak her name with gratitude." I cleared my throat. "They call her Gaia's healer."

I glanced at him.

"That is how I came to know Aconite."

We traveled south until the trees broke and cacti became our only respite from the Sun's glare. I'd soaked in the sun's warmth, basking in its glow for the first several hours, then sweat began to trickle down my back. Now, I lifted a hand to my forehead, shielding my eyes as I searched the horizon.

In a few hours it would be dark. And we still had quite a distance to go. My lips were dry after so long without water and the sun baking the moisture from my skin. I glanced at Firethorn who seemed to be faring far worse than I was. I had thought a creature of flame would relish the heat, but perhaps the cold truly was his element.

He stumbled, boots sinking into sand.

Overhead, I called a dark cloud, drawing moisture from the air. It blocked the sun, and soon, a light trickle peppered our skin. I sighed, the effects rejuvenating my sore muscles. Firethorn too, picked up speed, and he looked over at me.

"You're a lifesaver."

"Were you on the brink of death?" I asked in alarm.

He smiled and I looked away quickly.

"Do sea folk not have humor?" he asked seriously.

"Humor?"

"Jokes. A way to make you laugh."

I considered his words. "I find dolphin behavior amusing."

He barked a laugh. "I meant do you not tell each other funny stories?"

I frowned. "What?"

He stopped, turning to face me. "You've never heard a joke?"

I lifted a shoulder. "I believe I've answered your question twice."

"Perfect." He grinned. "My joke will be the first you've ever heard." He rubbed his chin. "I'll make it a good one."

His brows furrowed and he made several strange faces as I watched. Was this some form of the magic his mother was famous for? Would I be ensnared by it? Would my body be forced to comply? Dread crept in and I opened my mouth, but he spoke.

"Why do immortals make terrible storytellers?"

I hesitated, scenting the air for magic. "Why?"

"Because they never know when to end."

I blinked. My body had not responded. No magic.

"Do you get it? Because they're immortal... So they don't end."

I pressed my mouth into a flat line. "I do. But it's a fact. What makes it humorous?"

He let out a loud huff and kicked the dirt at his feet. "I'll keep thinking. I'm sure I can come up with something that will make you laugh."

I eyed him skeptically, but turned, resuming walking.

We walked in silence, the sun slowly sinking toward the horizon and I let my cloud dissipate.

Firethorn's stomach grumbled loudly.

I glanced at him. I wasn't entirely sure what his kind ate. He said nothing, continuing on as though he hadn't heard. "Should we… find something to eat?"

He kept walking, murmuring something to himself.

"Firethorn?"

"I've got it!" He spun toward me. "What did the ocean say to the beach?"

I stared at him. Was this another of his *jokes*?

"Nothing. It waves."

My lips tipped up and I pressed my fingers to my mouth. They had done it on their own. Magic? I sniffed. Nothing I could smell.

"How did you do that?"

He grinned and my lips curled up again. I had never met a creature who smiled as frequently as Firethorn. It was infectious.

"Well? Do you understand now?"

"I think so."

"Great! Try telling a joke of your own."

I pursed my lips. Something that would amuse him. Something about his muscles? Or perhaps his impressive height? I bit my lip, stepping over a shriveled cactus, now home to the insects after its long life.

"You are almost as tall as a tree." I searched his face for his reaction.

"And?"

I frowned. "And what?"

"What's the punchline?"

"Punchline? I thought I was telling a joke. Now we're telling punch… lines?"

He laughed.

"Ha! I did it. You laughed. I win."

Another smile crept on my face. I had beaten him at his own game.

We continued in silence and something shifted in my chest, light and unfamiliar. I had always been competitive, but this challenge, one of the mind, was more rewarding than a physical one. I would challenge him to another joke soon.

Next time, I would beat him completely. Then the pull came, low and insistent in my veins, the ocean closer than it had been an hour ago. I ignored it.

CHAPTER 12

Firethorn

In the pitch darkness of another moonless night, the tiny sparkling lights in the sky were brighter, more menacing. Their cold gazes bored into me, making my skin crawl. Somewhere, far from here, my home planet cooked under one of those suns, the last of my kind preparing to evacuate, to find refuge here.

What would Lorelai's father do when he learned more of my kind were coming? He had granted a mother and her children refuge, but what would he make of a hundred more? If that many still survived.

I turned my head toward Lorelai, stretched out on the large stone slab we'd stopped at for the night. I would have preferred we find cover—my reception outside Winter had not been too welcoming—but she was confident nothing would attack us while we slept here.

"Can't sleep?" she asked quietly.

"I was hoping you'd tell me another joke," I said.

Her mouth curved faintly. "You aren't ready for another of my jokes yet."

A soft chuckle slipped free. But as quickly as it had arrived, my mirth died.

I adjusted against the stone, bracing an arm beneath my head. "What will your father say when you bring me to the ocean?"

She twisted a lock of hair around her finger, and in the dark I could swear it held the shape of the thicker mane I'd glimpsed beneath her magic. "He will be pleased to meet you."

I snorted softly. "I doubt that."

"Why?" She released her hair. "He offered you and your mother a place to live. Why do you doubt him?"

Because I had seen what mercy looked like when it failed.

I tipped my face back toward the stars. From here, they appeared harmless. I knew better. I had seen what horrors they could bring.

Sixty years ago, all our seers' predictions had finally come true. Our sun, pulled by some force unknown to us, drew closer to our planet, increasing temperatures tenfold and killing most in a matter of months. Forced underground, the fae sent dozens of our kind out in search of a habitable world.

Mab swore she knew of a place created with her comforts in mind. Some laughed. Others avoided her altogether.

My father—the Creator—had visited our world twice.

Once, before I was born, staying long enough to draw the sun's attention. Or so the seers claimed. The second time, when our world was already dying, I was ten. It was my first and only glimpse of the being who made me. Some believed the seers and demanded he leave at once.

All feared him.

What would Mab say now to convince them to return with her to a world created by the one they believed had doomed us?

I turned back toward Lorelai. All of the hostility I'd encountered in Faerie had been from the land fae, and after our meeting with the satyr, I wasn't certain Oceanus ruled them. Lorelai had treated me with contempt too. Could it truly have only been because I'd burned a forest?

My attention drifted to her arm, noting a patch of scales. Those had not been there before. Was she changing? Weakening again without water? Or was she becoming what I most wanted to see?

I rolled onto my side, facing her. "Why did he allow us to stay?"

"My father isn't evil. Would he turn away a young boy and pregnant female?"

I had no answer. I only had my mother's stories. Should I tell Lorelai and her father? Prepare the king for their arrival?

I angled my face back toward the sky. We'd made our desperate escape fifty years ago. The memory felt distant, but I knew how long it had taken. Several months.

I had time.

I would learn what sort of male the king was first. If he was not the fair king Lorelai painted him to be, I would prepare to make plans of my own.

The third day was the longest.

Sandy dunes stretched endlessly in every direction, the heat pressing close and relentless. I'd stripped down to a thin silk top, my clothes clinging damply to my skin, the leather of my pants chafing with every step.

Lorelai's raincloud did little to help. Even the heavy droplets soaking me were warm, offering no real relief. If we did not find water and food soon, I feared I might sink into the sand and simply stay there.

"We're close," she said.

The words were the sweetest I'd ever heard. I imagined the wave that would greet me, the moment I could let myself fall into it and escape this tortuous heat.

A small leathery creature darted past us and Lorelai tracked it with her gaze. "Should we catch it?"

I stumbled through the deepening sand, licking my lips. "Why?"

"To eat."

I grimaced. "I don't eat flesh."

She frowned. "What do you eat?"

"Plants. Fruit. Nuts. Whatever the soil provides."

Her teeth were blunt like mine. I had assumed she ate as I did, but perhaps that was naïve. I searched my memory for any mention of kelpie sustenance in my mother's books.

Fish and seaweed.

I wrinkled my nose. None of the folk in my mother's court consumed meat, but many animals did. Did that make sea folk animals?

"When we reach the sea," Lorelai said, "I will have seaweed prepared for you."

I nodded. I was willing to try almost anything. Except flesh.

The sun tilted toward the horizon and I exhaled a fiery breath. The temperature was dipping, a welcome relief, but a new scent reached me. It was fresh and slightly minerally, like a breeze after rain. Ions buzzed and beside me, Lorelai's steps grew steadier.

We crested a hill and I gasped. Before us, an expanse of sparkling blue stretched into an infinite distance.

I stared, awe-struck by its might and beauty. I had never seen so much water in one place. "It's enormous."

Lorelai smiled. "This planet is nearly three-fourths water. The land makes up only a fraction."

I gaped at her. I had left my mother's corner of the realm, walking a day and three more with Lorelai. And I knew this world was far larger. Yet I hadn't imagined land only consumed a quarter of the planet. It was no wonder the king ruled this realm.

"Come. I will show you my kingdom."

We trudged through the sand that grew wet and firm beneath us and I stopped to remove my boots, feeling the sand between my toes. It was cool and spread, forming a trail of footprints behind me. I glanced back, mouth hanging open as the water absorbing my footprints erased all trace of my path in moments.

Lorelai's gaze met mine and I saw apprehension in her eyes. A thrill of terror shot through me, my heart speeding. Was it a trap? Was she leading me to my death? No. She could have killed me a dozen times. And yet. Underwater, I would be far weaker than I was on land.

Then, before my eyes, she shifted into a creature I had only seen sketches of. She towered over me, her violet seaweed mane whipping in the wind, and approached me slowly, kneeling down on one lavender-scaled knee and snorting.

I looked at her broad back, recognizing the same iridescent pattern I'd glimpsed along her arm as we walked.

"Do I... ride you?"

She blew out a breath through two huge nostrils at the end of a long snout. So.. yes?

Tentatively, I wrapped a hand in her mane, throwing a leg up and over until I was straddling her back. In kelpie form, she was three times the size of her fae form and I wrapped my other hand in her mane, squeezing my legs tightly against her back. I had either made the worst mistake of my life, or I was about to see a world I hadn't dreamed of.

She rose, taking off at a run that would have saved us days had she offered to do it sooner. But perhaps she couldn't take this form so far from her kingdom. I knew nearly nothing about her kind.

She raced into the water, but rather than sinking into its depths as I'd expected, her hooves kicked up spray and the water surged around us, carrying her across its surface. In moments, we were surrounded by frothing sea spray and open water stretched endlessly in every direction. I craned my neck to glimpse the shoreline disappearing behind us.

A creature burst from the water ahead of us, leaping high before diving back beneath the surface. Another followed. Then another.

Lorelai tossed her head, making a sound somewhere between a snort and a laugh.

"Dolphins?" I asked.

Her head bobbed once.

One skimmed the surface beside us, spraying my face with cold water before vanishing again. I laughed despite myself, leaning over Lorelai's back to splash at the space where it had been.

A chorus of clicks answered me, sharp and playful, and several shapes raced alongside us for a time, surfacing and diving in quick, fluid arcs.

I found myself smiling, the tension in my chest loosening despite the speed and the open water around us.

After some time, the dolphins dropped back and it was only Lorelai and me once more. The air was cooler here, the water darker. Below, it seemed to drop into a black abyss, and some of my elation died.

The king's castle would be far below the surface. How would I reach it?

She slowed and I glanced around. Water rolled in dark swells toward a horizon burning with the last of the sun. Soon, the moonless night would erase everything. Would I sink into darkness and never be heard from again?

Lorelai sank below the surface and I sucked in a great gasping breath.

She dropped like a stone, falling so fast the world blurred by. Pressure built behind my eyes and in my ears, but she continued to fall. My chest tightened as I fought the instinct to breathe.

I looked up, spying only faint streaks of blue overhead. Glancing down, a massive white structure materialized in the gloom. It seemed to be lit from within.

We dropped faster and I squeezed my thighs tighter to keep from slipping off her back and floating away.

Lorelai landed hard on a stone surface, her hooves clacking against stone as we moved through arched white pillars. My lungs had begun protesting and my heart sank as we passed inside the castle and realization struck. This was an underwater castle. For sea creatures.

It held no air.

CHAPTER 13

Lorelai

I picked up speed as Firethorn's grip on my mane tightened. I had overestimated his ability to hold his breath. The main halls were too large to clear in time. I had no choice but to race for my rooms.

I galloped down the halls, cursing my ignorance. I'd never brought a land creature to my court.

We reached my rooms and I shifted quickly, throwing out my hands, pressing all my strength into forcing back the water. Behind me, he landed hard on wet stone and gasped raggedly. I kept pushing until every corner of the room was filled with air.

He climbed unsteadily to his feet and took me in.

Ah. Clothes. I had forgotten that detail in my haste to save his life. I rarely shifted between forms in front of others and the clothing I'd lost this last shift were another in a long line of garments lost to the aether.

I slid past him, through the arched door where my air magic stopped and swam to a closet in the next room, tugging out turquoise fabric. I dressed quickly, stepping back through the door to my room and stopped.

Firethorn was standing beside my table, holding up a large piece of seaglass. He peered through it and set it down with the others.

I tucked a strand of hair behind my ear. "What are you doing?"

His lips quirked and my heart thrummed in my chest.

"Is this your room?"

I moved, scooping the pile of colorful glass up and sliding it inside a drawer. "Yes."

My father had made his expectations clear long ago. An heir did not confide. Did not soften. Did not feel the things that made you vulnerable to your enemies. I had learned early which feelings those were, and I had buried them accordingly.

Firethorn turned in a slow circle, taking in the sparseness of the space. It was true I spent little time here and with all my tasks, there was little time for hobbies or decorating, but it was my escape from the obligations of court. My one place to be myself.

He smiled. "I like it."

My cheeks cooled and I was sure they had paled. "Come. I'll take you to the kitchen."

I led the way out of my room, clearing a path for Firethorn and letting water collapse behind us. The majority of my court were sea folk without my shifter gift. Much as I wanted Firethorn to be comfortable here, I would not inconvenience them.

He caught up to me, walking beside me and a childlike wonder lit his face as he peered down corridors and into rooms as we passed. He was so unlike the male I'd heard of for half a century. He was curious, thoughtful. Interested in the world he lived in. Oceanus often said Mab had no desire to live in our world. That she would change it to suit her whims if allowed.

She was forced to remain in the frigid north, not only to protect the realm from her son's fire, but to ensure she did not force the land folk into submission.

I had seen Firethorn's power. A fraction of it, I was certain, but when faced with danger, he had chosen not to use it. The more time I spent in his presence, the more I wondered if my father had misjudged their kind.

We stepped in the kitchen and I formed a bubble around him. "I'll be right back."

He looked like he wanted to argue, but he nodded and I stepped through the bubble, into the water and searched for our cook. I found her in the algae storage room. She tugged a strand of mugweed down, pulling a large jar from where it floated overhead and reached up into it to pull out a pickled herring.

"Rill."

She turned to face me. "Lorelai! You've returned."

I pressed a kiss to her cheek. "I brought a guest. He survives on a plant based diet. Do you have something he can eat already prepared?"

She glanced over my shoulder, and an eyebrow shot up. "A land fellow?"

I pursed my lips. "Yes." Though I was sure my father wouldn't harm him, I had my doubts about some of the others at court. Rill was an excellent cook, but if I told her who I'd brought with me, the castle would know of it in no time. "I'll take whatever you have now and if you could send something to my rooms at dinner, I would be grateful."

She dipped her chin, peering around me again. It had been wise to leave Firethorn in the next room. I wasn't positive she would know what he was on sight, but it wasn't a risk worth taking. Many of the folk of my court had no experience with land fae and wouldn't know a fawn from a troll, but...

Rill grabbed another strand of rope pulling down a jar and reached inside, bringing out a handful of fermented seaweed. It was stained a deep brown from weeks in fungi enzymes. Though my tastes strayed toward fish, fungi gave the seaweed a distinct taste and my mouth watered at the sight. "Perhaps enough for two?"

She handed me the first handful and reached in for another.

Seaweed gripped in two fists, I stepped through my bubble, handing Firethorn his meal. Inside the air pocket, it wilted into a pile of limp strands and he raised a brow.

"It's better than it looks."

He hesitated only a moment before hunger got the best of him and he stuffed the seaweed into his mouth. I followed, chewing quickly and swallowed, licking my lips. Just as delicious as I remembered.

"Come. I'll show you more of my castle."

Every step at the very center of the sea restored more of my magic. The nauseous feeling settling in my stomach all day receded and magic funneled through me, calming the turbulent waves far overhead.

Down here, the magic restored itself. I should have felt relieved. I didn't.

CHAPTER 14

Firethorn

Columns the width of ancient trees vanished upward, their tops lost to darkness, while the floor stretched on in broad, uninterrupted sweeps of stone. We moved down hall after hall, stepping into room upon room and soon I was so turned around, I knew I'd never find my way. Sea folk swam past us, giving me a wide berth, but none seemed particularly afraid of me. Not like the land folk.

I found that although I was trapped within her air bubble, a prisoner with no way to escape, I'd never been more at ease.

Here, I was a stranger. Here I could be anyone.

We stepped into a large room, grander by far than the others. On the ground, far below the ceilings, I imagined the room filled with floating folk overhead. What was a floor to me, was of no consequence to creatures with no legs. I tipped my head back, craning to see more. To imagine.

"Would you like to experience it as one of my kind?"

I looked at Lorelai. Her hair was nearly dry after so many hours of exploring. Scales covered most of her arms now and her nose was longer. Was it because we were in her realm? Surrounded by her magic?

Not waiting for my reply, she held out a hand. "Will you trust me?"

The open earnestness in her eyes struck me. As if the question were vitally important to her. Did I trust her? I had trusted her enough to come to her court. To put myself at her mercy. I nodded slowly. "I believe I'm beginning to."

I slid my hand in hers and the bubble tightened until it was only around me.

I inhaled a shallow breath but my focus was immediately stolen by a long, shimmering tail wrapping itself around Lorelai's legs. Another glamour? Her magic? Did I want to see her as a mer creature?

She pumped her tail and we pushed off the floor. Up. Up into the expansive room until we hovered at its center. It took me a moment to orient myself as we floated.

She reached into the bubble, grabbing my other hand, and spun us in a circle. A soft smile touched her lips and I stared, mesmerized by the beauty of it.

"Lorelai, I—"

"Lorelai," A booming voice cut me off. I searched the dark depths of the room for the owner of the voice, but didn't have to wait long to learn who its owner was. In moments, a pair of snake like creatures slithered through water, lighting a path toward us, then two more and another pair behind them. They circled us, setting the room alight.

Behind them, a creature appeared, scaled in bright turquoise, long flowing hair the same shade. His scales coated nearly his entire body and a glimmering aqua tail cut through water.

He stopped, peering down at us. I didn't think it was an accident that he floated above us. Though I was certain I would have been taller than him on land, I sensed that to attempt to rise above him would be considered an insult.

He eyed me suspiciously and a crown of golden spikes glinted in the glowing snake-creature's light.

"Prince of Winter." His gaze ran over me. "Welcome to my kingdom," he said, but I no longer felt welcome at all.

Lorelai dropped one of my hands, spinning and placing herself between us. She'd said her father couldn't harm me. That he wasn't cruel. But her rigid posture said otherwise.

"I am honored to be welcomed by you, King Oceanus." I tried, awkwardly, to float around her and dip my chin to the sea king, but my feet were coming out from under me and his raised eyebrow said he was not impressed by my attempt at deference.

"Father."

"Clear the dining hall for our guest Lorelai," he said, cutting her off. His gaze fell on me again. "It was rude not to offer our guest an opportunity to refresh upon arrival."

He snapped his fingers and two kelpies appeared from the dark. "Take the prince to a guest room. Clear it of all water so he is comfortable. Find him something suitable to wear."

His last words were riddled with disdain.

Lorelai's mouth clicked shut and she said nothing as the first kelpie female thrust a hand through my air bubble and wrapped it around my arm. The second followed her lead, grabbing my other arm and I was dragged away.

Lorelai's eyes had narrowed on her father and they held all the turbulence of a storm.

I held my tongue. The sea king did not seem like a male who was used to being contradicted. I trusted Lorelai. More than I'd believed I would.

The king was another matter.

The kelpie to my right, dipped in midnight scales from head to toe, clearly had air magic. She funneled fresh air into my bubble as we moved and when we reached a room far smaller than any of the others I'd seen until now, she cleared the space of water, dumping me unceremoniously on the floor forming a solid wall in the arched doorframe.

The pair swam away without a backward glance.

I looked around the windowless room, spying a bed of seagrass splayed limply across the floor. There was no need for bars in a prison where water would hold me fast. And I was certain this *was* a prison.

CHAPTER 15

Lorelai

"How am I expected to gain his trust if you treat him so uncourteously?"

My father's gaze settled on me, unhurried. The chamber was vast, grown rather than built, its arched ribs of coral rising high above us. Light from the reef beyond filtered in through the open walls, fractured and restless.

Oceanus drifted closer, his great tail stirring the currents with idle authority as he set a heavy hand atop my shoulder. "You have more than proved yourself today, Daughter."

I stilled. "What do you mean?"

"A handful of days was all that was needed," he said mildly, "to convince our enemy's son to walk into my kingdom and surrender himself."

Ice slid down my spine.

"You can't harm him," I said quickly. "The bargain."

His gaze swept over me, sharp and assessing. "Have you grown attached to the male?"

My fingers twitched despite my effort to remain still. "No."

For a moment, he studied me. Then his mouth curved in satisfaction. "Good. Because now is the time to act. While Mab is off this planet."

The sea beyond the ballroom walls shuddered, responding to the sudden tightness in my chest. "She will be back, Father. What then?"

Oceanus smiled, two rows of sharp teeth catching the light. "Then I think she'll do just about anything to get her son back."

I drifted away from my father, tail cutting a sharp arc through the current as unease coiled tight in my gut. I had thought the prince from another world would be crude. Violent. A barbarian shaped by flame and conquest.

Instead, he had been patient. Curious. Careful with his words. Kind in ways that had caught me off guard.

And now I had delivered him into my father's hands.

The water around me grew restless, currents tugging harder with every breath. Beyond the palace walls, the sea surged against the reef, waves crashing in uneven rhythms that spoke of my faltering control.

Oceanus noticed.

"A queen must master herself," he said to my back. "Your emotions unsettle the realm."

I couldn't answer him. My throat was tight, my thoughts spiraling too fast to catch.

I turned and fled the ballroom, pushing through the palace corridors until the pressure in my chest became unbearable. By the time I reached my chambers, the sea was roiling violently outside the open arch, my magic thrashing in response to the sick weight of what I had done.

I sank onto the smooth stone ledge beside my alcove and forced myself to calm down.

My gaze fell to the table beside my bed and I opened the drawer. Seaglass. Dozens of pieces, each smoothed by centuries of tide and time. Firethorn had paused here in quiet fascination only hours before, lifting one piece carefully, turning it in the light as though it were something precious rather than discarded.

He would never trust me again.

He might never leave this place.

My father was not kind to his enemies. He was patient. Calculating. He waited centuries to settle debts.

I pressed my palms together, fighting the tremor. I could not let myself unravel—not yet. Not when I would have to face Firethorn again and pretend that nothing had changed.

When the summons finally came, my nerves were frayed raw.

The dining chamber had been cleared of water by the time I arrived, the floor dry and gleaming beneath the glow of Oceanus's light. Like Firethorn, his gift was flame. Not very useful under water, but he found ways to put it to use often enough.

My father sat at the head of the long table, shoulders straight, jaw tight.

To a casual observer, he would appear regal, in control. I knew him well enough to see the cracks.

Firethorn was already seated at his right. Something he said had unsettled my father. *Good.*

Firethorn did not stand when I entered. As princess, in my court, he should have shown more respect. But either he didn't know our customs or he intended to slight me.

Firethorn continued speaking as though I were not there.

It struck like a physical blow, nausea curling low in my belly. I kept my gaze fixed on the table as I crossed the room and took my seat, my hands clasped too tightly in my lap.

"What is your plan?" he asked evenly. "To keep me here forever?"

Oceanus lifted his goblet, swirling it in a slow circle. "Only long enough for your mother to make a new bargain with me."

The words settled heavily in the air.

I could feel the storm of thoughts rising inside me—fear, guilt, defiance, dread of what Mab would do when she discovered the truth. The water outside the chamber began to churn in answer, currents surging hard enough to rattle the reinforced walls.

My father's gaze flicked to me, sharp and warning. In front of Firethorn, he would say nothing. But the message was clear.

I lowered my eyes, my mind racing.

And all the while, the sea raged on, already sensing that something irrevocable had begun.

CHAPTER 16

Firethorn

By the time I was returned to my new room, I understood exactly how they meant to keep me contained.

The space itself was dry, the stone floor bare and cold beneath my boots. No fire. No comforts meant for land-dwellers. The walls curved upward into a domed ceiling, smooth and seamless, broken only by a tall window carved directly into the sea and a wide arched doorway that led into darkness.

Water pressed against the air in my room, black and endless. When I laid a hand against it, I could feel the ocean on the other side. Cold, crushing, alive.

The arched doorway loomed against the far wall, a living curtain of water filled the arch, flowing into a corridor already swallowed by the sea. One step through it and I would drown long before I ever found solid ground. No wards. No chains.

The ocean itself was the prison.

I could use my flame to melt the very stone around me, boil the sea if I pushed hard enough.

I could rely on the bargain Oceanus had made with my mother—he would not let me drown.

Or I could wait and see what came next.

Two nights passed with no food. No footsteps. Stone and sea. Nothing else.

I tried to rest, to plan, to count time by the faint changes in light filtering through the water.

Mostly, I thought about Lorelai.

She had been nothing more than a carefully placed lure and I had been hooked. The point of her dagger wedged deeply beneath my ribs. I had followed her willingly into the deep.

"Will you trust me?"

The words were laughable now. But I laughed only at myself.

Mother had warned me the sea folk were our enemies. Foolishly I had believed I knew better.

Every word out of her mouth had been a calculated lie. I had swallowed them whole.

I cursed myself for dwelling on it. For letting her live in my thoughts when she wasn't even here.

And yet the memory that kept returning wasn't a cruel smile.

It was the way the ocean had roiled when she lost control. She hadn't been able to meet my eyes at the table. Then, she had fled the room as though the weight of what was happening had made her physically ill.

I hated that it made me wonder.

Was it for me? Or had she truly been sick?

The ocean outside my window surged violently, waves slamming hard enough to make the stone vibrate. I turned toward it, jaw tight. Even trapped here, even betrayed, I found myself worrying about her.

On the third day, the arched doorway rippled.

A figure stepped through the wall of water as though it were nothing.

My heart lurched as I turned, but the creature standing in my doorway wasn't the backstabbing princess. A sea fae, sharp-eyed with deep navy scales rippling down his arms and legs inhaled a breath. *Shifter.*

One of the rare ones who could move freely between land and sea. Who could breathe where I could not. Who could walk the corridors of death beyond my door without consequence.

"I'm Neraxis," he said in greeting. "I know you've already seen a bit of the castle, but since this is your home now, I thought I'd show you more of the place."

Home. The word struck like a blade.

I forced my expression into something neutral.

"How is she?" The words were out before I could stop them.

Neraxis studied me for a moment before answering. "She struggles with the weight of her great responsibility."

My jaw tightened. I didn't care. It was dumb of me to ask.

Neraxis wrapped me in a tight bubble of air as we stepped into the hall.

I wasn't fool enough to believe he would show me anything of value on our tour, but anything was better than staring at bone-white walls any longer.

The castle was grand, pearl-veined columns and exquisite carvings lining every hall.

It was clear the king valued pretty things. I filed that away for later.

When Neraxis finally led me into the dining chamber that night, I nearly collapsed into the nearest chair. Hunger made my movements sharp, my patience thinner than I liked. But though food was already laid out, I made no move toward it.

If sea customs were anything like those in Winter, no one ate before the monarch.

Oceanus slipped through the air pocket, forming legs seamlessly, his gait unhurried as he sat at the head of the table.

"I trust Neraxis kept you entertained." He met my gaze, cool amusement on his face.

I remained silent, praying to the stars my stomach wouldn't give my desperation away as the scent of roasted seaweed and mushrooms invaded my nose.

Dark turquoise lips tipped up at the corner and he surveyed the spread. "I have no appetite. Perhaps a swim before we dine."

I ground my teeth, swallowing my pride. "The castle is quite grand."

He nodded and lifted a fork, set out for dinners with land dwellers no doubt, filling his plate with several items I couldn't name. It didn't matter. I would eat anything at this point.

Sweat dotted my brow as I waited, uncomfortably reminded of the nights I'd waited for my mother to arrive before eating. On more than one occasion, she'd failed to come at all.

Oceanus looked up, raising a brow. "It's not poisoned."

I hadn't considered that it was, but now my stomach soured. I lifted my fork, spearing items from the same dishes he had onto my fork and sliding them carefully onto my plate. His teeth caught the light as I looked up.

"Is this one of Mab's customs?" He raised a brow. "To wait for your host to dine?" Had I misread him? Perhaps he hadn't kept me waiting. I found I still had so much to learn about his kind. He didn't wait for my reply. "What did you find most appealing on your tour?"

I swallowed the grass like food in my mouth, clearing my throat. "The coral garden was breathtaking," I answered honestly.

He grinned, showing off two rows of sharp teeth. My mind drifted to Lorelai. In her true form, were her teeth as sharp? *The better to tear out my throat*, I thought bitterly.

He continued asking questions, quizzing me on his court, his folk. I answered. Short, succinct replies that bordered on rude. He didn't seem to notice.

"When will your mother return?"

My head snapped up. The niceties were over. My half-full belly churned. At last I would learn his true reason for trapping me here.

"My mother does not consult me on her travel plans."

A crack sounded and Oceanus spit a sharp tooth on the table. "Don't toy with me boy."

He believed Mab would bargain. Believed she would trade anything to have me returned. I did not correct him. I stared, straight faced, hoping he would read the seriousness in my expression.

"Then I suppose we have nothing to discuss."

He stood, sweeping from the room without a backward glance.

My gaze lingered on my plate and the piles of food set out. When would he call for me next? Days? A week? I stood, stabbing the nearest plate and stuffing jelly filled sacks into my mouth. They were a squishy consistency and tiny balls burst on my tongue. I had no name for the food, but the deliciously salty taste had me licking my lips and quickly stuffing the remaining morsels in my mouth.

Neraxis appeared in the door. "I must return you to your room."

His words were almost apologetic, but it didn't fool me. If I'd learned anything in the undersea, it was that water folk were masters of disguising their emotions.

"He'll release you if you tell him what he wants to know," he said as we reached the end of a long hall.

I ignored the shifter, stepping into my small room.

"Just think about it," he said to my back. I didn't turn. "He's been patient with you but the king is not one to wait long."

I curled my hands into fists.

Not known for his patience? Could the shifter not see he'd already played the long game. Offering us refuge in his realm. Bargaining with my mother for our safety. Biding his time for fifty years until she was gone before he made his move.

I wondered now if my first meeting with Lorelai had been an accident at all. I spun around. But Neraxis was gone.

When Neraxis came for me the following night, I was grateful for the certainty of food—and furious with myself for it.

Only when he led me back into the cleared dining chamber and I saw Oceanus already seated did the pattern finally sharpen into certainty.

I was only permitted to eat when it was with the king.

Another of his games.

The pattern repeated. Each day Neraxis brought me out, paraded me around the castle. Let the folk see me. Each night the king made polite conversation, asking me how I enjoyed his hospitality, his folk before the questions about my mother began.

But my comfort wasn't worth my court's safety.

On the sixth night, a messenger arrived mid-meal, water still clinging to his hair as he crossed the chamber and leaned close to Oceanus. His voice was low, urgent.

"The north is unstable," he said. "Wolves roam the forests. Killing and maiming. Polar bears push beyond their borders, slaughtering wild creatures."

Oceanus rose so abruptly his chair scraped across the floor. He slammed a fist down on the table.

"Stop this."

I lifted my gaze slowly.

"It will continue as long as I remain here."

Oceanus's eyes sharpened. "Is that a threat?"

I shook my head once, calm despite the tension coiling tight in my chest. "The creatures in Winter aren't under my control." I paused, watching understanding creep into his expression. "My mother's wolves sense my distress," I continued evenly. "They always have. They will continue to answer it until I am returned."

The room went very still.

And for the first time since I had been dragged beneath the sea, I saw the great king of the ocean hesitate.

Chapter 17

Lorelai

The waves raged on the surface, seeking vengeance. My magic swelled and sank, desperately trying to find that calming rhythm necessary to sedate the great beast.

It hollowed me out from the inside, a deep, bone-weary ache that left my limbs heavy and my magic trembling beneath my skin. The ocean answered every unsteady thought, every spike of emotion, surging and pulling until I could barely keep it from tearing itself apart.

I spent the first day curled in my bed, arms wrapped tightly around myself as riptides coiled outside the open arches of my chambers. The second passed in a haze of half-sleep and pain, my magic flaring and fading as I tried—and failed—to still the sea.

How long would Luna be gone?

The question surfaced again and again, useless and desperate. Her absence was too great, the balance she helped maintain a monumental task I could not achieve. I could feel it everywhere. In the tides, in the pressure, in the way the ocean no longer obeyed me as easily as it once had.

By the sixth day, stabbing hunger dragged me out of my rooms.

I hadn't answered my father's summons to dinner. Not once. I knew Firethorn would be there, seated at Oceanus's side like a prize already claimed, and I could not bear to face him.

The way he hadn't stood when I entered the room. The way he hadn't looked at me. The memory twisted like a blade in my chest.

I forced myself from my chambers at last, swimming slowly through the palace corridors, keeping my head down as court folk drifted past in tight clusters. Their voices carried easily through the water, hushed but urgent.

"Wolves," they said. "Whole villages"

"And the polar bears, Gaia help us."

I slowed, heart pounding.

"They're slaughtering everything in their path," someone murmured.

My breath hitched.

Mab's wolves.

Firethorn's wolves.

The corridor seemed to tilt around me as the truth crashed down in a suffocating wave. This was because of me. Because I had brought him here. Because I had let my father use him as leverage.

Because he had trusted me.

I didn't remember deciding to turn around. I only knew that my body was already moving, magic stirring painfully as I pushed toward the inner chambers of the palace, toward the one place I had been avoiding with my entire being.

Toward him.

Oceanus could not kill Firethorn. But he could keep him here.

Forever.

The thought clawed at my ribs as I swam faster, fear and guilt tangling until my thoughts blurred. I imagined Firethorn trapped in that dry room, cut off from the world that sustained him, paying for my betrayal with every breath.

By the time I reached his door, my hands were shaking.

I stepped through the arched threshold and let the shift happen, tail giving way to legs as my feet met the dry stone floor. The air felt wrong in my lungs after days submerged, each breath too thin, too sharp.

Firethorn stood near the window, his back to me.

"I came to—" My voice broke. I swallowed hard and forced myself to continue. "I didn't know. I swear. I would never—"

He turned.

The look on his face was cold enough to steal what little breath I had left.

"You didn't know," he said softly. "Or you didn't care?"

"I cared," I said, the words tumbling out of me. "I care. I didn't bring you here for this. I didn't want—"

"You wanted my trust," he snapped. "And you had it."

The truth of that struck deeper than any accusation.

"I didn't have a choice," I whispered. "My father..."

"You always have a choice," Firethorn said. "You decided I wasn't worth the risk."

"That's not true." I swallowed hard. "I was trying to keep you alive. I didn't know what else to—"

"If that's true," Firethorn cut in, his voice sharp as broken glass, "help me escape."

The room seemed to shrink around us.

"I..." My chest tightened painfully. "I can't."

The silence that followed was devastating.

Firethorn's mouth curved, not in humor, but something bitter and resigned. "Then the killing will not end."

I stared at him, heart pounding, my mind scrambling for something—anything—that would make this make sense. This wasn't the male I'd spent days with. This wasn't the one who had listened more than he spoke, who had taught me jokes.

He wouldn't do this.

He couldn't.

I turned away before he could see the tears gathering in my eyes, before he could see how completely undone I was.

I'd seen the truth in his eyes, a moment before his resolve had hardened. He was hurt. *I* had hurt him. But this wasn't his doing. As I fled the room, one truth anchored itself painfully in my chest.

Firethorn was not responsible.

This was Mab.

It had to be.

And that meant there was only one thing left for me to do.

I had to go to my father.

I had to beg.

CHAPTER 18

Firethorn

Seeing her again was worse than I could have dreamed.

I had imagined a dozen ways to hurt her back. To make her feel even a fraction of what I had endured.

Instead, when she stood in my doorway, all I felt was a tangled knot of sadness and dread.

I was angry.

I was bitter.

And despite myself, guilt crept in anyway.

For the land folk dying because of me. For the certainty that the slaughter would not stop while I remained trapped here.

Oceanus would not free me to save them. He was like my mother in that way. Principled, he would say. Strategic. Unmoved by collateral suffering.

In the middle of it all, my traitorous mind took stock of Lorelai.

The dark circles beneath her eyes. Her wild hair knotted and unbound. She had lost weight. I could see it in the sharpness of her cheekbones, the way her clothes hung a little too loosely on her frame.

Her hands trembled when she clenched them into fists.

That, more than anything, nearly undid me.

I reminded myself that she was my enemy.

Caring for her would only weaken me.

She left more shaken than when she arrived.

I was alone again.

That night, Neraxis never came.

I stared at the open door. The long corridor stretching into darkness.

At first, I thought it was a delay. Another quiet cruelty meant to keep me guessing.

I waited.

When thirst clawed sharp and painful, I pressed my palm to the wall of water, cupping my hand against the window and letting the cold seep into my skin. It wasn't enough. It quenched my thirst, but no amount of water would ever be enough to fill the hunger.

The days blurred.

No one came.

The sea beyond the window raged on, indifferent and endless.

And I understood, finally, what Oceanus intended.

CHAPTER 19

Lorelai

The night I left Firethorn's room, racing down the long corridor toward my father, I had one goal in mind, make him see reason.

One of the court spies, the only one I trusted, Vaelor, intercepted me, his expression drawn and urgent. He bowed low. "Your highness."

I searched his wide eyes and tugged him into a private room. "What is it?"

He scanned the darkness for prying eyes and I did the same, sending a wave of water out and testing its bounds. The nearest member of court was out of earshot. "Tell me."

He dipped his chin. "Your father is mounting his army."

Relief swept through me. I had misjudged him. He would quell this threat and keep the people safe.

"They march on Winter's border in two days."

I grabbed his shoulders. "To stop the wolves?"

He searched my face. "No highness."

I released him, backing up. My father wasn't stopping it. He didn't care about the land folk. He saw an opportunity to attack his enemy when her defenses were spread thin and he was taking it. Did he have a plan for her wards? He must. Nothing could get through them without her permission.

"Report to me first," I told him, my voice steady despite the tightening in my chest. "Before my father."

He hesitated only a moment before nodding.

Over the next two days, reports came in fragments. Wolves roaming far beyond their territories. Polar bears crossing borders they had never breached before. Villages razed. Innocents slaughtered.

The sea above the palace raged, winds tearing at the surface hard enough that even below, the currents churned violently. The ocean mirrored my unrest, tides pulling and recoiling as if something ancient had been provoked and would not be soothed.

I chewed my nails until they were raw stubs. Could I get Firethorn out? Would the killing stop if I did? Or would he turn that wild pack of wolves on me and everyone I cared for. Even without his fire, they were unstoppable. Not truly alive.

I grabbed my stomach, wrapping my arms tightly around my waist as pain spasmed through my middle.

I couldn't wait any longer. Couldn't let the suffering continue while I sat by. The ocean's might answered to me. I had the power to stop this.

I swam for the surface, breaking with a wave that stretched into a sky darkened by rain and black clouds, and dove again, swimming below its turbulent surface for the beach.

Dragging myself ashore, I shifted into kelpie form and galloped at speed for satyr territory. I followed the trail of destruction inland, letting instinct guide me where reason failed, until the forest swallowed me whole.

I lifted my nose. Coppery blood salted the air.

I stepped into the clearing and halted, shifting quickly.

Antemysa lay crumpled at its center, her throat torn open, green soaking into the leaves beneath her. I rushed to her side and pressed my hands against the wound, desperate and useless, trying to hold together what was already slipping away.

Her breath rattled wetly. Her eyes found mine.

"Kill him," she choked. "End Mab's heir before Mab returns." Her fingers tightened weakly around my wrist. "Please."

There was no saving her. The terrible certainty of that truth sank into my bones.

On my knees in the dirt, blood warm beneath my palms, I lifted my face and begged any one of the deities to hear me. "Gaia," I whispered. "Please. Stop this. Kill the wolves. End it." My voice broke. "This is my fault. I lured the prince into my father's trap. I did this."

The forest stilled.

She stepped into the clearing as though she had always been there. Gaia's presence was vast and grounding, ancient as stone. "Rise, child. Do not bow to me."

I pressed my head to the mossy floor. "Please mother. Help us. His wolves will end them all."

Gaia laid a gentle hand on my shoulder. I kept my head pressed to the earth.

"I have raised his sister," she said. "I have seen the goodness their kind *can* possess. In this, only Oceanus is to blame."

I sat up, tears streaming down my cheeks and opened my mouth to argue. To beg.

Then I saw her.

A shy female knelt beside Antemysa's body, her hands shaking as she pressed them to torn flesh, whispering frantic words in a language I did not know. Magic spilled from her—strange and raw and *alien*—nothing like the powers of this world, yet desperately trying to bring life back where it had already fled.

Silver hair spilled down her back, bright in the afternoon sun and eyes like cut emeralds were focused on the fallen satyr leader. Firethorn's sister. Their similarities twisted my gut.

She pressed bright palms against Antemysa's ravaged neck chanting faster.

Antemysa did not breathe again.

The girl's shoulders shook as the truth settled in.

I rose slowly, the weight of everything pressing down until I could scarcely breathe.

"Go, child. Do what must be done."

Numb, I dipped my chin and stumbled away, my thoughts racing like gusting wind in my head and Gaia's words a drumbeat against my skull.

CHAPTER 20

Firethorn

The first time I heard the water slosh, I thought it was a mistake.

Lorelai losing her hold on her magic. A sea fae passing too close. Anything but what it became.

The sound came again. Heavier. Closer.

I turned toward the doorway just in time to see the wall of water bulge inward, as if the sea itself had decided to lean into my room.

The line on stone disappeared, the space eaten as it crowded closer. Unhurried. Like it had all the time in the world.

I backed up until my shoulders met the wall beneath the window. Water lapped at my boots. Then my shins.

A week without food or a single familiar face had been its own kind of torture.

But the week that followed was worse.

The water rose to my waist. My chest. My throat.

I braced myself, hands splayed against slick stone as the last pocket of air shrank around me.

My lungs pulled in one final breath, thin and precious, and then the sea swallowed the room.

I kicked and thrashed, fighting instinct, fighting panic, fighting the awful knowledge that there was no surface to reach. My fingers found the doorway's watery veil and pushed through, desperate.

The corridor beyond was a tunnel of dark water with no light at the end.

Death.

I jerked back, choking on the truth and the pressure in my chest. I tried to hold my breath. To be a deity's son instead of a male trapped in a room with no air.

My lungs lost the battle.

I gulped.

Water, cold and crushing poured into me. My eyes bulged. My chest convulsed, screaming for breath. Pain lanced through my ribs and into my throat, bright and merciless.

And then—

The water began to recede.

I fought to hold onto consciousness even as I spasmed in my weightless tomb. It receded inch by inch, leaving me collapsed on stone, coughing and retching until blood flecked the water at my lips.

I lay there shaking.

It took minutes for my lungs to heal. For the burn to dull.

Just long enough for me to believe it might be over.

Then the slosh came again.

And again.

And again.

Each time, I prayed it would be the last.

Each time, the sea rose like a patient executioner.

Each time, I drowned.

By the end, I couldn't tell which was worse, the moment my lungs surrendered, or the moment the water retreated and left me alive to wait for the next.

When the doorway rippled and a figure stepped through the veil, I didn't have the strength to rage.

I lifted my head from the stone and stared at my executioner. Finally, I would be free of the unending torment.

Lorelai stood over me.

I dragged in a shallow breath that still tasted like seawater and blood. "Will it be you, then?" My voice scraped over bloody vocal cords. "Come to twist the knife a final time?"

Her face crumpled.

"I'm so sorry, Firethorn," she whispered. "I didn't know."

I stared at her for a long moment. I should have felt hate. But I only felt relief. Too empty to even muster up betrayal.

With a resigned sigh, I shifted upright and bared my chest.

"I only ask that you make it quick."

Chapter 21

Lorelai

"No."

The word ripped out of me before I could soften it.

I crossed the room in a rush, dropping to my knees beside him. His skin was too pale. His lips carried a faint bluish tint that made panic claw up my throat. I grabbed his shoulders and shook him.

"Get up," I demanded. "I'm getting you out of here."

His gaze dragged to mine, heavy-lidded, hollow. "I won't be your puppet." His voice was ragged, bitter. "I've had enough drownings to last ten lifetimes." He swallowed hard, jaw tight. "Find a knife. Or some poison. I won't drown."

"I'm not killing you." My throat burned. "Firethorn, I know you have no reason to trust me. I know I don't deserve..." I cut myself off, because begging for forgiveness could come later. If we survived. "Please. Get up."

He stared at me for a long, brutal moment, searching my face for the lie.

I held still. Let him look. Let him see what I couldn't put into words.

Finally, he lifted a hand.

My breath hitched. I caught his fingers in mine and pulled hard.

"I can't breathe out there," he rasped, glancing at the water-wall in the doorway.

"I know," I whispered.

Then I did the only thing I could do.

I rose onto my knees, cupped his face with shaking hands, and pressed my lips to his.

I breathed into him, my magic sliding in beside it, like a current slipping under a door. I felt the moment his lungs accepted it, my magic swirling inside him. Ready to usher him out of this realm and back to safety.

His eyes widened slightly.

"Hold on," I breathed. "Don't let go."

I shifted into my kelpie form, motioning for him to climb onto my back.

He was weak. Too weak. But he'd have to do this part himself if he wanted to survive.

He struggled to his feet, swaying and leaning against my leg. Slowly, he climbed onto my back with what little strength he had left, fingers wrapping around my mane. His thighs squeezed and I couldn't help but compare it with the last time, when he was full of life and vitality. Now, he was a broken shell.

I surged through the doorway.

The sea hit us like a fist.

Above, the surface was chaos. Wind screaming, waves slamming, the entire world churning with rage and grief and guilt. I broke through the waves, bursting up in a spray of foam and rain, forcing all my magic into calming the ocean.

His grip slipped. I felt it, the sudden slack of his fingers, and my heart lurched into my throat.

Hold on, I thought, sending a surge of current backward, bracing him with the force of the sea itself. *Hold on, Firethorn.*

We raced for the rocky shore closest to Winter.

Behind us, the water shifted.

A line of shadows rose from the deep. Soldiers, moving fast, cutting through the sea with the relentless coordination of predators. My father's army.

They had seen me.

I pushed harder, muscles burning, magic scraping raw as I sent wave after wave behind us, slamming walls of water into their path. It slowed them, but it didn't stop them. Nothing truly stopped an army that belonged to Oceanus.

The shore loomed ahead. Jagged stone, slick with rain, unforgiving and sharp. I surged onto it anyway, hooves striking rock. I raced over wet soil, then grass, not slowing until the mossy carpet of the mushroom forest disappeared beneath a thin blanket of snow.

Firethorn slid from my back, collapsing hard onto the ground.

I shifted fast. Hands, legs. Dropping beside him and dragging him up by the arm.

"Up," I panted. "Breathe. Just breathe."

We lay there for a heartbeat, both of us heaving, rain cold on my skin, the ocean roaring behind us like an angry god.

Then soldiers broke from behind the tree line, one after another. They marched over thick tree roots and briars, eyes fixed on us with single-minded intent.

I staggered to my feet.

I lifted my hands to the sky and called down my fury.

Lightning cracked across the sky, white and violent, striking the trees between us and the advancing soldiers. The shockwave rattled my bones. The smell of scorched air and ozone filled my lungs.

I grabbed Firethorn's hand and hauled him upright.

"Come," I gasped. "We have to get to Winter."

He swayed, barely standing, but his fingers tightened around mine.

"They can't cross her wards," I whispered, as much prayer as promise.

And then we ran.

CHAPTER 22

Firethorn

Winter's border rose from the storm like a promise I no longer believed in.

The air changed first. Sharper. Cleaner. The world pulled tight around itself as my mother's wards called me home like a beacon. Almost there. On the other side I would be safe from the sea king and his army.

Snow gathered in thin sheets across the ground, clinging to rock and root, muffling the world until even the storm felt distant.

Lorelai staggered beside me, her grip tight around my hand.

Each step burned. My lungs still ached, every breath a reminder of wet and darkness and the way the sea had taken me apart piece by piece. My body remembered what my mind tried to forget.

At the edge of the ward line, I stopped.

Her fingers tightened. "We're almost there," she breathed, hope fragile and raw in her voice.

I turned to face her.

She was a mess of mud-streaked skin, hair clinging to her face in wet tendrils and bruises everywhere a tree branch or bramble had struck her as she raced through the wilds of Faerie.

I let my nails lengthen, the magic answering me easily now that I was closer to home. Claws curved sharp and sure, familiar as breath.

Her eyes widened.

"You didn't really think," I said quietly, "that I would trust you again."

I drove my hand into her stomach.

She made a small, broken sound, more surprise than pain, and sank to her knees in the snow.

I stepped back, chest heaving.

"I won't let you into my kingdom," I said hoarsely. "Not after what you did."

She looked up at me, blood staining her fingers as she pressed them to the wound.

"Firethorn," she whispered.

I turned away.

Each step toward the invisible border was heavier than the last, but I forced myself forward. Forced myself not to look back. I crossed the line, the magic sealing around me like a warm blanket as I stepped across.

Then I heard it.

A howl.

I stopped.

Another answered it. Then another. Shapes moved through the trees, pale eyes gleaming as shadows circled where she knelt alone in the snow.

"Firethorn!" she cried.

Then she screamed.

The sound tore through me. My feet were already moving before I knew I'd made a choice.

The wolves barely had time to react before I was on them, fury and fire ripping loose. I drove them back with a roar that split the night, chasing them into the trees until the forest swallowed their retreating forms.

I dropped to my knees beside her.

Blood soaked the snow. Too much. Far too much. The wolves knew exactly where to bite to kill.

"No," I breathed, pressing my hands over the wound at her throat. "No, no, no."

Her eyes fluttered, unfocused.

I scooped her up without thinking, her weight terrifyingly light in my arms, and ran.

The wards opened for me.

I crossed them with her cradled against my chest, snow and blood blurring together as I tore through the night toward the healer's hall.

"Don't die," I begged. "Please. Don't die."

I stood in the doorway while the healers worked. Her blood had dried blue on my palms. I turned my hands over and looked at them for a long time, like they belonged to someone else. The room was warm. The fire was steady. Outside, the storm was still screaming.

I waited.

CHAPTER 23

Lorelai

I woke wrapped in warmth.

Thick woolen blankets weighed pleasantly across my body, the air scented with smoke and pine. Firelight flickered against stone walls, its crackle soft and steady, nothing like the roar of the sea I was used to.

For a moment, I didn't understand where I was.

Then memory slammed back into me.

I gasped and pushed myself upright, hands flying to my throat. My fingers brushed skin, unbroken, tender but whole. I sucked in a sharp breath and pressed harder, as if I could will the pain to return and confirm I was real.

"You're awake."

Firethorn stood in the doorway.

The sight of him stole what little breath I had left. Alive. Watching me with something guarded but unmistakably relieved in his eyes.

"You saved me," he said quietly. "I returned the favor."

The words steadied my terror, calmed the memory of nails digging into my flesh. His back as wolves closed in around me. Teeth sinking in.

And then I noticed it.

The constant pull on my magic was gone. The ache that had lived beneath my skin for weeks. The strain of holding the ocean in check.

It was too quiet.

I frowned. "Something's wrong." Panic fluttered in my chest. "I can't feel the sea. If I don't go back, it will ravage the land."

Firethorn crossed the room in a few long strides and sat on the edge of the bed, close enough that I could feel the heat of him. He handed me a mug, steam curling upward.

"Drink," he said. "Slowly."

"I can't stay here," I insisted, tossing the blankets aside. Pain lanced through me, the remnants of my nearly fatal wound still evident in the sluggish throb of my pulse.

"The sea has been restored," he said, eyeing me as I fell back against the pillows.

My heart stuttered. "What do you mean?"

He watched me for a moment, then spoke. "When we crossed into Winter, a wave swept over the land. It wiped out my mother's wolves. And many of the land folk." His jaw tightened. "For several hours, it was chaos."

The mug trembled in my hands as I tried to sit up again.

"Then Luna returned," he continued. "She brought the entrance to the mountain down behind her, but she restored the rest of Faerie. Commanding the ocean to return to its home."

The room seemed to tilt.

"She told me," Firethorn said more softly, "what you were carrying for her while I was your father's prisoner."

I exhaled a slow breath, my body finally giving in to exhaustion now that the danger had passed. My breathing slowed. The firelight blurred at the edges of my vision.

"And my father?" I asked.

Firethorn's mouth thinned. "He is threatening to send the ocean to level Winter if I do not return you."

The calm shattered.

I bolted upright, steaming liquid sloshing over the side of the cup and onto the blanket. “He will do it. He won’t hesitate.”

Firethorn set a steadying hand on my thigh. “Relax.”

I stared at him. “I can’t.”

“He can’t cross my mother’s wards,” he said firmly. “Not without our consent. You are safe here for as long as you want to remain.”

The words sank through my terror-soaked skin.

Safe.

"So," I whispered, "I'm not your prisoner?"

His gaze held mine. "No."

I searched his face for the trick. The catch. The unspoken cost. I couldn't find one.

"Okay," I whispered.

I don't know if he heard me. My eyes were already closing, the warmth of the fire and the weight of the blankets pulling me down into something that felt, impossibly, like safety.

I slept.

CHAPTER 24

Firethorn

I showed her the kingdom the way one does with something fragile.

Not the borders or the armories. I took her to the quiet places. Snow-laced paths through evergreens heavy with frost. The frozen river that cut through the valley like a silver vein. The high ridge where Winter watched the world without needing to touch it.

She walked beside me, careful at first, as if she expected the ground itself to betray her.

I listened.

Not with my ears. With the low, constant awareness I had always carried of those rare few who had found their way past my guard. Her heartbeat had been erratic when she first crossed the wards, a frantic thing that told me she was braced for pursuit, for punishment, for the moment my mother's protections would fail.

Day by day, her pulse softened.

It steadied in the mornings when she woke to frost instead of surf. It slowed when she realized no one was coming for her. It evened out when she stopped flinching at every distant sound.

That was when the truth settled uncomfortably in my chest. She had not been free in her father's kingdom. Not any more than I had been.

Luna's words came back to me often in those weeks, unbidden and unwelcome.

She chose to save you even knowing it could mean giving up her crown.

Lorelai had helped me escape and it may have cost her her crown. Her kingdom.

I had trusted Lorelai, and that trust had delivered me into a prison of unimaginable suffering.

And I had stabbed her.

The fact that she still walked beside me at all felt like a kindness I had no right to expect.

We fell into a rhythm.

She rose early, restless, wandering the grounds as though memorizing escape routes. I visited the mines, working to restore what Luna's mountain crossing had destroyed. I didn't bring her with me on those trips. Not yet ready to trust her with those secrets. I sensed my mother's impending return. Tasted it in the air.

When she returned, she would be angry. The wolves were gone. I had to restore the mines. That at least would placate her.

Lorelai greeted the low fae by name, learning their tasks, their stories. She sat with the dwarrow when they came up from the mines, dining with them and allowing them to braid her hair.

I wondered how she looked to them. What they saw when they sat with her.

She'd ceased appearing high fae long enough ago that I scarcely remembered the female I'd first encountered in the wilds. Her face had the same shape, her eyes still dark and inquisitive, but all her fae features had dissolved, leaving behind the scaled beauty who fit so well in my world.

She could have left.

That was the thing that unsettled me most.

Winter's wards would not have stopped her. I never once told her she had to stay.

And yet she did.

A dark, insidious part of me waited for the moment the blade came out. The moment she unveiled her final plan. But with each day that passed, she grew stronger, and soon there was no reason for her to remain in my court.

Winter was always cold, but certain times of year brought heavy snow and early nights. The dwarrow would need salve for their dry, cracked skin as the chill tightened around us like a noose. They were afraid of the rock trolls. I never minded going to get it. Before.

Leaving the protection of Winter's wards had been increasingly on my mind, though. I could not remain behind her invisible walls forever. One blustery morning, I started for the wilds beyond our border.

Lorelai's scent hung in the air. She'd watched me pack a bag in silence.

I turned back.

"Would you like to come with me?"

Lorelai looked up from where she sat, surprise flickering across her face before she masked it. "Outside Winter?"

"Yes."

She stood, pulling her cloak tighter around herself.

I didn't rush her.

We reached the edge of Winter before the sun had reached its zenith. Lorelai exhaled a long sigh as the sky cleared, snow settling on the branches. The moment we stepped through, I felt it. My mother's magic loosening its hold. The world sharpened, suddenly aware of me in a way Winter rarely was.

This was where she could run.

Where she could turn on me.

I gripped the knife tightly, refusing to turn and look at Lorelai as I knelt to cut the plant from the damp earth.

The silence stretched.

No footsteps retreated. No blade flashed.

She remained where she was, watching the tree line, not me.

When I rose, she was still there.

“Is that all you need?” she asked.

I nodded.

Before I could take a step toward Winter, a chittering erupted at our feet.

I stilled.

A line of SnapDragons had placed themselves directly in our path, their scaled petals spread wide, iridescent gold and blue catching the pale light. One marched to the front of the line and crossed his petals over his stalk, puffing a small cloud of smoke through his nostrils.

"You owe us a favor, Prince."

Lorelai glanced down, then up at me. "Friends of yours?"

"Acquaintances," I said carefully.

The SnapDragon's eyes narrowed. "We guided you. We were promised repayment."

"I haven't forgotten," I said. "I just haven't decided what to offer yet."

Another puff of smoke. "We have waited long enough."

I reached into my pocket, fingers closing around one of the gemstones from the mines.

The SnapDragon tracked the movement and his expression told me exactly what he thought of that offering before I even produced it.

I let it go.

Lorelai had gone quiet beside me, her gaze moving slowly over the line of creatures with the particular stillness she got when something had caught her attention and she was considering it.

"How far does your network stretch?" she asked the SnapDragon.

His eyes slid to her with open suspicion. "Far."

"From the sea?" A pause. "To the edge of Winter, yes?"

She looked at me then, and I saw it, the thing turning behind her eyes. "Your mother's wards protect us inside Winter," she said quietly. "But outside them—"

"We're exposed," I finished.

She nodded once. Then she crouched, bringing herself level with the SnapDragon.

He regarded her with something between wariness and curiosity.

"What if the favor wasn't a thing," she said. "What if it was a purpose?" He said nothing, listening. "There are those who would come for us in Winter," she continued.

"Forces that do not belong here and do not come in peace. You already watch and guard. What if you were named for it? Formally. By the Prince of Winter himself." She glanced up at me.

I understood what she was asking and crouched beside her, the moss cold and damp beneath my knee.

Around us, the rest of the line had gone motionless, petals closed, waiting.

"This is my bargain," I said. "And this is how I pay it." I held his gaze and let my voice carry the full weight of what I was offering. "I name you guardians of the realm. Go where the need is greatest. Take orders from none but the purest of heart. Let none who would do harm go unchallenged."

Tension in my chest uncoiled.

He stared at me for a long moment. Then he drew himself up and dipped his head in a bow so slow and deliberate it could only be called ceremonial. The entire line followed.

When he lifted his gaze again something had changed in his expression. The imperiousness remained, but underneath sat something older. Something that understood what it meant to be entrusted with a thing that would outlast everyone present.

"We accept," he said.

The line dissolved back into the undergrowth without another word, gold and blue winking out between the roots until the forest settled back into silence.

I stayed crouched a moment longer.

Lorelai rose beside me, brushing moss from her knees. When I looked at her, she was watching the tree line, her expression unreadable.

"You're that confident you're a better male than my father?"

I stilled. Then I looked at her more closely.

The corner of her mouth twitched ever so slightly.

"Did you just make a joke?"

She turned and started walking toward Winter. "I don't know what you're talking about."

I rose and followed, something loosening in my chest.

"My father's reach is long," she said quietly, after a moment. "And patient."

She had not said it as a warning. She had said it the way one speaks a truth they have been living with for a long time.

"Then it's good we have guardians," I said.

She glanced at me, her gaze softening.

We crossed back into Winter without a word, the cold settling like a familiar weight.

Evenings became quiet affairs. Shared meals taken in companionable silence. Long stretches where we spoke of nothing at all. When she did talk, it was often of the sea, her childhood and all that she'd given up.

She didn't say it was because of me.

She didn't have to.

"Why haven't you returned home?" I asked one evening.

"That's not my home anymore," she said. "Father does not forgive betrayal."

I swallowed, that small ember in my chest dimming. She wasn't my prisoner, but the bars were no less thick between land and sea.

"Your father tried to get you back."

Her eyes met mine. In them sat the particular exhaustion of a child who has never once been enough. "He didn't come for rescue."

Each night, I lit the fire in her chamber before retiring to my own. Winter nights were unforgiving, and she was not built for the cold.

More than once, I lingered in the doorway, watching the firelight catch in her hair as she curled beneath heavy blankets, her breathing slow and even.

One morning, I knocked softly. “Lorelai?”

I pushed the door open just enough to check on her.

She was still asleep. Curled on her side, hair spilling loose across the pillow, one hand tucked beneath her chin. The fire had burned low, embers glowing faintly, casting her face in warm shadow.

For a long moment, I stood there.

Then my hand reached for the charcoal. I hadn’t intended to draw, but somehow, I felt steadier with her so close.

I sketched quickly. The fall of her hair. The quiet vulnerability of sleep.

When I was done, I folded the page carefully and slipped away before the sound of her stirring reached me.

CHAPTER 25

Lorelai

I woke to the faintest trace of him still in the room.

Smoke and frost and something deeper beneath it. Not unpleasant. Not unfamiliar anymore. I lay still for a long moment, breathing it in, letting myself believe, just for this brief moment, that I belonged here.

The castle was quiet when I rose. Morning light filtered through high windows, catching on stone glazed with ice. If it had been natural, I might have set a chunk beside the fire and let it melt so I could draw the barest magic from it. But this ice belonged to Mab. My father had warned me of her gift. Her ability to sense a thing's true name and use that name to bend it to her will.

The proof was in the frozen walls that sparkled in sunlight but never dripped.

Oceanus had been wise to hide the realm's true name from her. With it, what terrible things might she have done?

I wandered the halls without purpose, tracing carvings, memorizing turns. There was beauty here, sharp-edged and deliberate.

The dining hall was already warm when I stepped inside. Firethorn sat at the long table where we broke our fast each morning, but now he wasn't alone. The folk of his court moved freely around him. Dwarrow, ice trolls, fawns whose names he knew. They spoke to him without fear. Laughed, even.

He listened.

The ease of it struck me harder than any display of power. I had assumed so many things about him when I found him in the wilds that first day. I was not the monster I'd been sent to tame.

How different it all might have been if I had let him show me who he was.

I left him there to conduct his day's work and continued exploring. The castle was not as large or grand as my father's, but it was no less beautiful. I hugged the oversized coat that had appeared in my room the first morning closer and blew out a frigid breath.

If I could find water, the magic would surge in my veins, helping stave off the cold.

But the rumors were true. Mab had frozen every stream and lakebed, cutting off all access to the sea.

I leaned against the wall, staring out at the vast ocean of white. Its smooth dips and curves were a gentle contrast to the restless surface of my home. It looked serene, but the biting cold was no less deadly.

My gaze snagged on a head of silvery white hair nearly the same color as the snow. I pressed closer to the glass, wiping away my breath-fog just in time to see him pause beside a polar bear. It lifted its wide black nose and bumped his palm before crouching low to allow him onto its back.

I ducked away as they circled and vanished into the trees.

I envied his freedom to move through this realm without fear of Mab's magic or the cold.

I had saved his life and handed over mine in the same moment. Now, I had only borrowed warmth and a court that tolerated me because he asked it to. Firethorn said I was not his prisoner. He meant it. But meaning something and it being true were not always the same. The wards kept my father out, but that was its own kind of prison.

That night, he didn't come to light my fire.

I waited longer than I should have, the chill settling deep into my bones. When the hearth finally went cold, the bite of ice clawed into my lungs. I wrapped my blanket around myself and stepped into the corridor, following instinct more than memory.

Though I knew where his chambers were, I had never crossed the threshold before.

The door yielded easily.

Inside, the fire burned high, heat rolling through the room in steady waves. Firethorn lay asleep on the bed, brow furrowed, breath uneven. The flames surged and dipped in time with him, restless and bright.

I understood at once.

Fire answered his emotions the way water answered mine.

He murmured in his sleep.

"No. Please. Can't breathe."

My heart twisted.

I crossed the room quietly and settled into a velvet chair, holding my hands out to draw in the warmth.

My gaze snagged on a folded piece of paper on the table beside me. I hesitated. This was his private room. It could have been a letter. Something not meant for my eyes.

I lifted it anyway, glancing once toward the sleeping prince before unfolding the page.

The drawing stole the air from my chest.

It was me.

Not as I had ever seen myself. Not as my mother had looked. Not as I imagined myself to be. This was truer than memory. Scales like moonlit water. Eyes dark and knowing. A creature shaped by tide and depth.

Was this how I truly was?

My gift had always been to show the world what it most desired. A reflection, not a truth. But this—

I folded the page carefully and set it back where I'd found it.

I rose and moved closer to the bed.

He had driven his hand into my stomach and left me for the wolves. I had told myself for weeks that I understood it. That grief does terrible things. That I had done terrible things too. That we were even. Standing here, looking at what he'd drawn, I finally stopped telling myself and simply believed it.

In sleep, his face was smooth, free of the deep furrow that marked him when he thought I wasn't looking . There was something achingly beautiful in the curve of his mouth, the quiet steadiness of him.

I brushed a strand of hair from his face.

His eyes flew open.

He tensed instantly, watching me as if braced for betrayal. As if waiting for the moment I proved every fear right.

"I'm cold," I whispered quickly. "Could you relight my fire?"

He studied me for a long moment. Then he nodded and rose without a word.

My chamber was freezing by the time we reached it. He coaxed flame back into the hearth, but even as it caught, the cold still sliced my lungs with every breath.

"It will take time," he said quietly. "For the cold to leave you." He hesitated. "My room is already warm. You can sleep there if you wish. I'll find another."

I nodded, shivering.

When we returned to his chamber, he lingered in the doorway while I climbed into his bed. His scent and heat wrapped around me at once, my stiff limbs finally loosening. I exhaled, long and slow.

He turned to leave.

"Wait." I pulled the blankets up higher. "Don't go."

He searched my face. Whatever he saw there softened something in him.

At last, he crossed the room and lay down beside me. The bed was large enough that my covers weren't disturbed as he slid underneath on the other side.

"I still taste it sometimes," he said quietly. "Sea water in my lungs."

I slid closer, until the warmth of him was all either of us could feel. I inched nearer, tucking my feet into the pocket of heat he created without thinking.

"He used to bring me to negotiations," I said quietly. "To sit beside him while he doled out commands. No one ever argued." I pressed my fists against my thighs and told him anyway. "I never knew what face they saw. Only that it worked."

His voice rumbled against my side. "Did it ever end?"

"He sent me to you."

I closed my eyes.

On his table, folded carefully, was the first true image of me in existence.

CHAPTER 26

Firethorn

They arrived like a storm breaking open the sky.

More than a hundred high fae poured into Winter with my mother at the helm, their magic colliding with the wards, the air, the silent stillness I had found in Mother's absence. Voices echoed through halls that had once known only the contented hum of workers. Power pressed in from every side.

My kind.

I had forgotten how loud they were.

Mab stood among them, flawless and terrible, her presence bending the space around her as it always had. Her eyes swept the castle with quick precision. The fractured stone. The scars Luna had left in the mountain. The empty ridgelines where her wolves should have been.

She didn't ask questions. That was not her way.

I found myself back in my chambers without remembering the walk there. The door closed. The noise dulled. My breath came easier.

Lorelai was there. I'd left her sleeping that morning, intent on preparing a new room for her, one with a larger fireplace, when my mother's arrival had set me off my task. I hadn't yet processed what happened last night. She'd slid next to me, curling into my side and fell asleep in moments.

I'd lain awake for hours unsure why I wasn't worried for my throat when it had been only a few weeks since I'd nearly drowned in her father's prison. The dream I'd woken from, my lungs spasming under the weight of all that cold water, had brought a fresh wave of terror. When I woke to find her standing over me, my first traitorous thought was that she would finish what she had started in the ocean.

But she'd saved me in the end and it wasn't fear I felt when I found her watching me at breakfast or in the halls.

She turned toward me from her perch beside the fire, concern softening her expression, and for a moment the chaos outside ceased to exist.

"I should go," she said quietly.

"No." I interrupted. "Don't."

I exhaled a long breath. "My mother has returned. It's... loud out there."

She studied me, then nodded, as though she understood more than I'd said.

"We can stay a while." The blanket wrapped around her slid down her shoulders, exposing violet scales.

I stepped closer, reaching for the blanket to slide it up, her lips tipped up, but the light in her eyes, like her scales, was dim.

"Lorelai," I backed up. "Are you unwell?"

I had wondered for some time now if the weakness in her stance, the sallowness of her skin were more than a slow healing wound.

Her soft smile faded and she turned to face out the window. Her hair fell down her back, tangled and bed rumpled. My hands itched, straining toward the strands. I wanted to drag my fingers through it, tame the unruly curls.

"I've been away from water too long," she whispered.

I felt how much the admission cost her. She was trusting me with a weapon.

Grabbing her hand, I tugged her toward the door. "Come with me."

Her grip was weak and my heart beat too hard in my chest as I pulled her faster.

Using tunnels rather than the main hall, I took her beneath the castle, down into the old mining chambers the folk had cleared of all gemstones long ago. The stone there was carved wide and smooth, the walls veined with the scars of gems long since emptied.

Releasing her hand, I called molten flame, feeding it into the wall. I whispered the words I'd overheard my mother say too many times to count, forcing the natural world to comply. They were some of the few she'd allowed me to remember.

It trapped my flame, pressing it through rock and fusing it with the very fibers of the substance until my lava and the rock's core were one and the same. Droplets began to trickle down warm rock. Soon, ice from the mountain flowed freely, filling the stone circle at our feet—to our shins, our knees.

Lorelai let her blanket fall, sinking down into the steaming water. Even only soaked to the waist, her scales glowed, lighting the liquid in a bright purple sheen.

I dropped beside her, kicking off my shoes and tossing them over the lip of the stone.

Steam curled upward, filling the chamber. I glanced over, my heart filling to bursting at the look of contentment on her glowing face as her head tipped back against the wall, eyes closed.

"It's yours," I said. "Your sanctuary from this cold, brittle kingdom."

Lorelai lifted her head, her gaze tracing the room before landing on me. "Thank you."

The relief on her face was immediate and visceral—her shoulders loosening, breath shuddering as warmth embraced her. She sank lower, water lapping at her collarbones.

The magic struck my chest hard enough to make me wince and icy stillness gripped me despite the balmy water.

I went very still.

A bargain. But she hadn't. She'd only said thank you.

“Lorelai,” I said quietly.

She hummed in response, eyes half-lidded.

“Can I ask you something?”

She opened her eyes, turning toward me. “Of course.”

“Tell me something about yourself.”

A faint smile curved her mouth. “That’s an odd request.”

“I know.” I met her gaze, holding it. “But I need you to trust me.”

She searched my face. “When I was young,” she said after a moment, “I used to love to come ashore and lay out on the sand. To feel the granules of sand between my fingers and toes as the sun warmed my skin. Oceanus would have been so angry if he knew.”

The pressure eased. The magic lifted its claws from my heart, satisfied.

Lorelai inhaled sharply, touching her chest. “What was that?”

“A bargain,” I said.

She sat up, splashing water in my face as she slid against the far wall.

I held a hand up. “It has released you, Lorelai.”

She stared at me, breathing a little too fast. “I didn’t agree to anything,” she said.

“I know.” My voice came out rough. “You didn’t mean to, but that doesn’t matter.”

Her brows knit together. “Firethorn—”

"In my world," I said quietly, "we learned early what bargains really are." Steam curled between us. "They aren't contracts. They're offerings. To the stars. They feed on them. When a bargain is broken the stars collect the payment."

Silence stretched.

"My mother taught us that the hard way. She made a deal with them long ago. It gave her the ability to take what she wants from others — whether they understand what they're giving or not."

Lorelai’s face had gone pale.

“So when you told me something true about yourself,” I said, “the magic heard, and the bargain was fulfilled.”

I swallowed. “But you must never do that again.”

"Thank someone?" she asked softly.

"Make a bargain," I corrected. "Not with my kind. Not with anyone."

She nodded. "I won't."

Then she splashed me.

I startled as water soaked my hair.

She laughed. I forgot what I'd been telling myself for weeks.

I stared at her, caught between disbelief and something far more dangerous. I slid closer.

Her hand brushed mine.

My breath caught.

The world narrowed to the space between us. The steam. The shared warmth.

I had spent weeks telling myself I didn't want this.

That I couldn't.

Fuck it, I thought and I wrapped my hand in her damp hair and pulled her to me.

Her gasp barely had time to form before my mouth found hers.

The kiss wasn't soft.

It was desperate. Starved. Everything I had swallowed down crashing free all at once.

Her lips parted for me, warm and yielding, and I kissed her deeper, needing more. Needing to feel her.

She made a small sound against my mouth, fingers clutching at my shoulders as she kissed me back just as fiercely.

The water around us began to bubble.

I drew her closer, forehead resting against hers when I finally pulled away, breath uneven, heart hammering.

For a long moment, neither of us spoke.

Everything we were too afraid to say hung between us.

CHAPTER 27

Lorelai

I woke stronger.

Not healed, but the ache in my bones had softened, and the tight, dizzy weakness that had plagued me since leaving the sea had loosened its grip. I could breathe without effort. I could stand without swaying.

And still, my thoughts kept returning to his mouth on mine.

The kiss had not been like anything I'd known before. It had felt like a pull, deep and insistent, as though something in my chest had shifted toward him and refused to be dislodged. I had spent the morning trying to name it, and failing.

That frightened me more than the weakness ever had.

I had spent so long being useful to my father, to the sea, to the balance of things, that I had never once stopped to consider what I wanted simply because I wanted it. Here I was useful to no one. I had no court to manage, no tides to hold. I was myself. I was not entirely sure I knew who that was.

By dusk, I dressed carefully. I chose fabrics that clung lightly to my shape, colors deep enough not to mark me as fragile. If I was to be seen tonight, I would not look as though I needed guarding.

A knock sounded at my door.

When I opened it, Firethorn stood, blocking the light, dressed impeccably for dinner. Regal and entirely too aware of himself.

"Did you dress for me?" I asked lightly.

"For you. Always." He leaned forward, pressing a chaste kiss to my cheek.

"I'm still getting used to this," I admitted.

His mouth curved faintly. "So am I." Something in me stilled. His expression tightened. "There's something I should have told you sooner," he said as we began to walk.

I waited.

"My mother did not come alone."

The words landed hard. I felt them settle somewhere just beneath my ribs.

"How many?" I asked.

"Enough," he said quietly.

"My father will be furious."

I looked down at our joined hands. Then I slipped mine free.

Lifting my chin high, I pushed the doors wide and stepped inside.

The dining hall he led me to was not the one we'd shared before. This chamber was vast, its ceiling lost in shadow, its walls carved with odd symbols that pulsed faintly with power. The moment we entered, conversation stilled.

Every eye turned toward me as I entered, Firethorn on my heels.

Mab sat at the head of the table, immaculate and terrible, her gaze sharp as it swept over me.

Firethorn moved to stand beside me. "Mother. This is Lorelai."

I didn't miss the way he avoided my title and my court.

I stopped at the empty seat closest to his mother and Firethorn gave me an odd look as he stopped at the seat beside me.

Mab's smile did not reach her eyes as we sat.

A high fae seated beside me leaned close, murmuring something in a language I didn't recognize. I turned toward him, raising a brow in confusion.

Firethorn tipped his head toward me. "He asked if the sea has always been so bold as to send its daughters uninvited."

Ice flared in my cheeks.

Before I could reply, Mab's voice cut cleanly through the room, sharp and amused.

"There's no need to trouble yourself with translation," she said. "It is past time the low fae learned a more cultured tongue."

The blank faces at the table told me they didn't understand her, but I did. That cut had been meant for me alone. I glanced to Firethorn who was frowning up at his mother.

I forced myself to eat, though the vegetables were strange and dry on my tongue, their flavors foreign and dull compared to what I knew. Curious stares burned my neck, my face. I did not shrink from them, meeting the eyes of any who were bold enough.

At the end of the meal, Mab rose and spoke again, her words flowing in the unfamiliar language of their kind. The room hummed with anticipation.

Firethorn leaned close, his warmth a balm to my nerves even though my insides twisted at his betrayal. "There will be a ball."

Around the room, everyone pushed back their chairs, leaving plates half full. We were ushered into an adjoining hall where voices rose in song, haunting and beautiful, though I understood none of the words. The music twisted through the air, shaped by a high fae standing near the dais, her hands weaving sound itself into form. Lights bloomed overhead, scattering like stars across the ceiling.

Pairs formed quickly, laughter and silk moving together.

"I need to speak with you," I whispered, tugging Firethorn's arm.

He nodded, letting me pull him into a dark corner of the room. He searched my face. "Lorelai, I'm sorry. Truly. I should have told you sooner."

Pressure built behind my eyes, and I inhaled a slow breath. Had anyone ever apologized to me before?

"No more secrets. Please."

He dipped his chin. "Agreed."

He held out his arm, but before I could decide whether I would take it, someone caught his sleeve, pulling him away into the crowd.

I stared after him, chest too tight. When he didn't return, I moved to a low table at the edge of the room, watching the magic unfold. This world was brighter than mine, louder, its language and customs unfamiliar.

Mab appeared at my side as though she'd always been there.

“I know who you are, Lorelai,” she said softly. “Princess of The Sea.”

My stomach twisted.

“What I don’t know,” she continued, “is how you found your way into my son’s bed.”

The words struck like a slap. A chill rose in my cheeks. The sudden, sharp awareness of how I must look to them.

"He has always loved the wrong things," she said. Almost to herself. "Broken things. Strange things." She eyed me. "It never ends well.”

I straightened.

“The bargain you made with my father does not extend to your new court,” I said evenly. “I hope you have a plan to keep them safe. When he learns of this, he won’t be pleased.”

Mab’s smile sharpened.

I turned and left before she could reply.

She didn't call after me. She didn't need to. We both understood: I remained in this castle because she permitted it. The moment that changed, no ward in Winter would protect me.

I kept my pace steady until the hall swallowed me, until the music faded behind stone and distance. Only then did I run, skirts gathered, breath burning, until I reached the safety of my room and closed the door behind me.

Only then did I let my hands shake.

CHAPTER 28

Firethorn

I saw her leave the hall.

Not quickly enough to draw attention. Not slowly enough to be graceful. She moved with her head high and her shoulders squared, and I knew—*knew*—that whatever had driven her out had teeth.

I followed.

By the time I reached the corridor, she was already gone, the echo of her steps swallowed by the vast open corridor. I stood longer than I should have, listening to the music bleed faintly through the walls behind me. My mother's court had filled the castle with sound and light and false cheer.

And I'd never felt so different. In a world where I had always been the outsider, I suddenly wondered if I would ever belong anywhere.

I stood outside Lorelai's closed door.

I knocked.

She opened it with surprise flickering across her face, then something softer. Relief, perhaps. Or resignation. I couldn't tell.

"I thought you might—" I stopped myself. The words shifted. "I thought you might sleep in my room tonight."

The careful composure she'd worn all evening cracked just slightly. "All right."

We didn't speak as we walked. The castle walls crowded closer now, the halls buzzing with too many folk; too much noise. Every shadow seemed to lean closer, listening. When the door closed behind us, the quiet pressed in hard enough to make my chest ache.

She sat on the edge of the bed, smoothing her skirts. I removed my jacket and set it aside, suddenly unsure where to look or stand.

I moved closer, close enough to touch, but kept my hands fisted at my sides. She was a refugee in my kingdom. That didn't mean she wanted me.

She looked up, dark, fathomless eyes met mine and my fingers lifted as if drawn by her magnetism, tracing the line of her jaw.

She leaned into the touch as though she'd been waiting for it, the tension in her shoulders easing and my heart pounded.

I sank onto the bed, sliding back until my head met the headboard and held up an arm.

She scooted toward me, moving until she was tucked beside me, curling at my side, her head settling against my chest.

I exhaled a shaky breath. Having her wrapped against me felt natural in a way nothing else had.

The memory of her mouth on mine flared hot, but I kept my hands still, fingers splayed against the blanket. She breathed slowly, evenly, as though matching her rhythm to mine.

“Firethorn,” she said quietly.

“Yes?”

“I saw her.”

My heart stuttered.

“Who?” I asked, though I already knew.

“Your sister.”

The world narrowed to a single point beneath my ribs.

“I searched for her.” My breathing hitched. “I couldn't find her and then...”

"She's alive," Lorelai said firmly. "She's with Gaia. She's helping the folk. Healing them."

I closed my eyes, the weight of years apart pressing down all at once. Hope, sharp and treacherous, surged through me, and with it, fear. I had told myself she was out of reach.

"I need to find her," I said.

Lorelai shifted, propping herself up on one elbow. "Then we will."

I frowned. "The wards—"

"I can cross them," she said. "But not unnoticed. If we're going to do this, we'll need Gaia."

A ripple of unease ran through me. "Oceanus—"

"When I prayed, she answered," she said. "If we cross into the forest quickly, quietly, she may answer again."

I stood, pulling on my boots, offering Lorelai my hand. She took it without hesitation.

The forest beyond the castle was cold and dark, the trees bent beneath frost and age. The wards resisted us at first, as though Mab's return had prompted them to hold me, but I was a part of Faerie. Both Mab's heir and my father's. I pressed harder and felt the magic give. Together, we slipped through.

The moment we set foot in the moss-covered forest, Gaia appeared as if from nowhere.

She stepped from the shadows, more alive than any creature I had yet encountered.

"You have finally found each other," she said eyeing us both. "And now you search for me. Why?"

"My sister," I said hoarsely.

A shape moved behind her.

A high fae female with long silver hair broke from the trees and crossed the space between us in a heartbeat, her arms wrapping around me with crushing force.

For a moment, I couldn't breathe. She was too solid, too warm, her weight real against my chest in a way memory had never been. My hands came up on instinct, gripping her shoulders, then her hair, as if she might dissolve if I loosened my hold. She was tall compared with the other high fae at court, but not nearly as tall as me. Nothing like the infant I'd last seen half a century ago.

My knees threatened to give out beneath me as fifty years of searching, of failing, of believing I'd broken her beyond repair crashed through me all at once. I bowed my head against hers, a sound tearing free from my throat that wasn't quite a laugh and wasn't quite a sob.

"I'm so sorry," I breathed.

"I never blamed you," she said fiercely. "Not once. I am happy here."

When she released me, I told them about the high fae. About my mother. About the court swelling in Winter.

"I want to bring her," I said, meeting Gaia's gaze. "Just once. So she may see her kind."

Gaia was silent for a long moment.

"Twenty-four hours," she said at last. "No more."

Relief hit me hard enough to leave me dizzy.

When I turned back toward the castle, Lorelai stood beside me, her hand brushing mine. Her presence steadied me and for the first time, I returned to my mother's court with a lightness in my step.

CHAPTER 29

Lorelia

The moment we crossed back through the wards, the forest's magic shuddered, like a held breath released too quickly. Firethorn walked at my side, Aconite between us, her fingers curled tightly around mine. She was quiet, eyes wide as she took in the castle rising ahead, its spires sharp against the winter sky.

I felt him before I saw him. *Neraxis.*

He lingered at the tree line, half-shadowed, water-slick hair plastered to his head, eyes too knowing to be anything but deliberate. The king's assassin did not hunt without purpose.

My steps didn't falter.

If he had come for me, he would not strike while I was flanked by a fire prince and a goddess-blessed fae. And if he had come for Firethorn... *No.* I would not think it.

For twenty-four hours, all that mattered in the world was Firethorn's sister. I would do or say nothing to jeopardize their time together.

He hadn't come to kill anyone. He'd come to remind me that he could. For the moment, Neraxis was safely on the other side of the wards. I would deal with him later.

The court swallowed us whole the moment we entered. Eyes followed Aconite with open curiosity, whispers skating just beyond my understanding. Like me, she did not speak the high fae tongue. Like me, she smiled anyway, chin lifted, daring them to underestimate her.

I didn't leave her side. I felt a strange kinship with the high fae who had been raised in Peloria since birth. Like me, she was foreign to these creatures. Other.

When we reached the long hall, Firethorn squeezed my hand, staring at me over Aconite's head. "I need to find her a room and get her settled in for the night."

I nodded, smiling warmly at his sister. "I will see you in the morning."

She beamed at me, wholly unafraid, and I envied her courage.

I could have returned to Firethorn's room. His open invitation lingered long after he'd departed with his sister, but tonight I gave him some long overdue time with Aconite.

Alone in my room, the image of Neraxis's cold gaze burning into me lingered behind my eyelids. If I went now, he'd be expecting me. I wasn't foolish enough to believe I had escaped my father's wrath. Still, Neraxis was Oceanus's best assassin for a reason. Only a fool let him see them coming.

That night I slept alone, tossing in the heavy blankets, and dreamed of slick hands, red with Firethorn's blood. When I woke, a cold sweat drenched my back.

The day passed quickly, Aconite's name whispered in the halls by both the high fae and the folk who had been brought in to serve them. I eyed the land creatures for any sign of coercion, mistreatment, but found none. It appeared they chose this, though I couldn't fathom why.

Firethorn smiled the way he had when we first met.

Before my father.

Before my court took his softness.

I slipped away to the Hot Springs, determined to recharge my magic before the evening and dressed quickly for the ball. It was to be a celebration of Aconite's return to her court, a reminder that one day, she would rule by her mother and brother's side.

I stared up at the gaudy display, reminded of my father's extravagance and pressed my lips flat to avoid a scowl.

Music threaded through the hall, woven by magic I could not name. Lights bloomed overhead, bright enough to blind. Firethorn stood beside me, Aconite to my left, her grip tightening when the press of bodies grew too close and I squeezed back in reassurance.

Mab moved faster than I expected.

She swept in, grasping Aconite's hands and pulling her free with practiced ease. "Come, child," she said warmly. "You must be seen."

Aconite looked back at me, eyes wide.

Firethorn was there in an instant, stepping between them. "Mother."

Mab's smile sharpened. "Dance with your sister, Firethorn."

I swallowed, preparing for her next barb when my two companions disappeared, but Firethorn turned to me instead and held out a hand. I glanced at his sister, but she gave me an encouraging smile.

His hands were warm when I took them, steady and sure. The music swelled, and he guided me onto the floor with a confidence that stole my breath.

He was radiant.

I had seen him strong, furious, restrained—but never this. Here, among his people, he fit in a way I never would. The court moved around him like a living thing, recognizing its own.

The truth settled: I did not belong here. But the shape of it was different from what I had always known. In my father's court I had always known my place. I had simply never been permitted to be anything beyond it. Here, I did not belong — but I was visible. Myself. The difference was not nothing.

"If you keep looking at me like that," he murmured, "I'll start to worry."

"I need to see my father," I said quietly. "To beg for his mercy. To return home."

His steps faltered.

The music carried us through the turn, his grip tightening. Silence stretched taut between us.

"That's a death sentence," he said at last. "I won't let you go."

The truth was, I didn't want to go. But how could I ever fit into his world?

I scoffed softly. "So I'm your prisoner now?"

The words struck him like a blow, his face going pale.

"No," he said hoarsely. "Never. If you truly want to return to the sea, I won't stop you. But you told me yourself. Your father does not forgive." He cleared his throat. "And I know what he's capable of."

My heart sped, pounding hard. When had this male truly forgiven me? When had I become precious to him? I surged forward and crushed my mouth to his.

For a heartbeat, he froze, then his arms wrapped around me, fierce and unyielding, holding me as though the world itself were trying to tear us apart.

The eyes of his court burned my back and I pulled back, wrapping my hand in his and tugging him off the dancefloor.

He didn't ask where we were going. We wove silently through the crowd of narrowed eyes and vicious glares as we made our way to the exit, my heart in my throat.

Chapter 30

Lorelai

In his chambers, the fire burned low and steady, casting shadows across his face.

My skin prickled as I let the gown fall off my shoulder. His eyes were dark as they devoured every inch of me and for the first time in my life, I knew it was the real me he saw. Not a reflection. Not a face shaped by someone else's wanting. Me. I burned under his stare in a way I hadn't known I was capable of.

The fire cast warm gold across his bare throat, the strong line of his jaw, the faint scar at his collarbone I'd traced once in idle curiosity and never forgotten.

I took a step toward him. Then another. Each one deliberate.

When I reached him, I slid my hands into the front of his shirt, gripping the fabric as though anchoring myself to something solid in a world that had never once been kind.

"Tell me to stop," he whispered.

"I won't," I said. "But I'll never take what you don't offer."

I rose onto my toes and kissed him. It was slow. Searching. A question pressed mouth to mouth. I had kissed before. I had never kissed like this. Like it mattered what the answer was.

His hands came to my waist, wrapping me in a security I had never known until now.

When he kissed me back, it was with a reverence that made my chest ache, as though I were something precious. As though I mattered. I didn't know what to do with that. I kissed him deeper instead.

I slid my fingers into his silken hair and felt the shudder he didn't bother hiding.

The soft, unguarded sound unraveled me. He wasn't performing. Neither was I. I couldn't remember the last time that was true.

He trailed soft kisses down my neck, the heat in his tongue sending shocks through me that resonated all the way to my center.

"Firethorn," I breathed. He smiled against my collarbone, soft lips moving south.

His mouth moved to my jaw, then my throat, then lower still, each kiss unhurried, lingering, as though he were memorizing me the way I'd memorized the scent of smoke and frost that clung to him.

I tugged at his shirt.

He obeyed without a word, pulling it over his head and discarding it somewhere behind us.

His heart beat beneath my hand, strong and unrelenting. I wondered distantly how someone so powerful could be so gentle when he could have taken whatever he wanted from this world.

He cupped my face, pressing his brow to mine.

"Lorelai." He murmured my name and my heart leaped in response to the sound of it on his lips. Not princess. Not sea creature. Not Oceanus's daughter. Just me.

I kissed him again. Deeper.

Need unfurled low in my belly, a slow gathering tide.

I reached for him, backing up, and he followed, letting me command him.

The bed met my knees. Then my back as I sank into the mattress, dragging him down with me.

He hovered above me, searching my face. His body pressed into mine, solid and anchoring. The weight of him. The firelight. The way he was looking at me like I was something worth looking at.

I slid my hands along his shoulders, down his arms, mapping the breadth of him, the strength of him, the male who had never once tried to cage me.

Then he stilled.

The change was subtle. A tension in his shoulders, a shift in his breathing. Not hesitation exactly. Something more honest than that.

"I don't know what I'm doing," he said quietly. The admission cost him. I could see it in the set of his jaw, the way he held himself carefully still above me as though bracing for the blow of my response.

Something warm and certain moved through me.

I had spent my whole life being whatever a room needed. A reflection. A tool. A face no one could say no to. I had given and performed and bent myself into a hundred different shapes for a hundred different rooms.

Nobody had ever handed me this.

The power of it was almost dizzying.

I pulled him down and kissed him slowly, deliberately, until I felt the tension leave his shoulders. Then I rolled us over, sitting up astride him, and looked down at him in the firelight.

"Then I'll show you," I said.

His throat moved. His eyes were very dark.

I showed him.

A shout of pleasure and surprise burst from my lips when his teeth closed over my sensitive nipple. At the same moment, two fingers slid inside me, finding a rhythm that unraveled me.

"Firethorn," I gasped as he increased his pace.

He slid up my body, lips claiming mine in a kiss that stole my breath and divided my focus between his skilled fingers and his delicious mouth.

He was a fast learner. Attentive in the way he was attentive to everything, watching my face more than anything else. Not my body. My face. As if what was happening to me was more interesting to him than anything else in the room. I had never had that before. I hadn't known it was something I needed.

His hands were careful in a way that had nothing to do with inexperience and everything to do with who he was.

"Tell me if I hurt you," he said.

I pulled him closer instead of answering.

He reached my neck, kissing along my jaw, then lifted to search my face once more. "Tell me."

I exhaled the exasperated huff and released his hair, sliding a hand down the sharp cut of his stomach to the impressive length between his thighs and gave it a tug. "Are *you* unsure?"

He gave a strained laugh, but allowed me to guide him to my entrance.

His eyes never left mine as I tugged him closer, sliding a hand along the hard length of him.

I stopped thinking about what I was risking and simply felt it. Him. The weight of him. The heat. The way he held me like I was both precious and necessary, and I understood for the first time that those two things were not in conflict.

Not releasing him, I wrapped an arm around his back, hugging him to me, needing him closer. My hand slid lower, drawing a broken sound from his throat. I lifted up, capturing his lower lip between my teeth. His kiss was desperate, breathless.

I released him, rolling my hips to the movement. My head fell back.

I don't want to be alone anymore.

The thought arrived without warning and I didn't push it away.

I called out his name again, the pressure that had been building finally giving way, my thighs wrapping around him, moving in perfect unison, until he fell against me panting.

"I would do anything," he breathed against my mouth, "to hear my name on your lips each and every night for the rest of my life."

I kissed him instead of answering.

It was answer enough.

Whatever this was, it was irreversible. I didn't know when the line between us vanished. Only that I had never felt so present. Or so completely his.

I slept pressed to him, memorizing the weight of his arm around my waist, the heat of him at my back.

When dawn came, pale and unwelcome, I knew what I had to do.

"He will kill me for this," I said softly, the words steadier than I felt. "But if Neraxis brings word to his court, it won't be only me who pays."

Firethorn stirred beside me, but didn't wake.

I pressed my lips to his cheek, stealing a bit of his warmth before wrapping myself in one of his thick coats and tiptoeing lightly across the room.

I wasn't leaving him. I was leaving for him.

There was a difference, even if he'd never know it.

CHAPTER 31

Firethorn

I woke to the cold. Not the bite of Winter. Something worse. Emptiness. My hand closed around nothing. A scrap of paper lay where her head had been. I recognized it immediately.

My drawing.

I turned it over with shaking fingers.

The ink was uneven, hurried, the letters wide and looping.

Firethorn,

You were the first to ever see me as I truly am. For that, no matter what life brings, I will be grateful.

There was a spy in the woods. One of my father's. I've gone to stop him before he can bring harm to you or to Aconite. I must try to make things right with my father.

I found something here I didn't know I was missing. The other half of my soul.

Don't be angry. If Luna wills it, I will return to you.

For now, cherish your sister. She is a treasure meant to be kept safe.

And be careful with your mother.

—L

I flipped the paper back over.

The lines of my drawing stared up at me, the curve of her jaw, the sweep of her hair, the quiet strength I'd tried and failed to capture. My palm flattened against it, as if I could hold her there through ink and memory.

Grief clawed through me. Fear followed close behind.

Aconite was still here. Safe for a few more hours before Gaia's time ran out. I wanted nothing more than to go after Lorelai, to drag her back behind the wards in Winter where she would always be safe. But I was no jailer. For now, I would cling to the hope that she would return to me.

I dragged myself from the bed and went to find my sister.

Aconite was awake, already dressed, her hair loosely bound, her expression bright as she turned toward me.

"Did you enjoy the ball?" I asked quietly. "The court?"

She smiled, softly. "I prefer sleeping under a different canopy each night. There are always people who need help. Those who benefit from my herbs and healing."

Of course she did. My kind, big hearted sister. As I'd always known she would be.

We clasped forearms and walked together toward breakfast.

The hall buzzed with voices when we entered and she straightened her shoulders. She didn't know the language of the high fae. In truth, it was still a strange distant memory nestled at the back of my mind, but I'd had ten years in our home world and Mother often rattled off words in her native tongue when her anger got the best of her.

I pushed carrot around my plate, my appetite gone as the memory of my night with Lorelai replayed on a loop in my mind. Her soft moans, my name on her lips, long, dark waves tangled in my fingers as I tugged her head back and kissed the tender skin at her neck.

I startled from the memory of her smooth calf resting in my palm when a shrill cry cut through the room and a female leaped to her feet and threw herself into a male's arms, laughing and weeping all at once.

Aconite leaned toward me. "What is happening?"

"She's found her mate," I said watching the pair.

"Mate?" She stared at me.

My mother rose, her voice carrying easily through the hall. She spoke of bonds formed only between high fae. Two souls inexplicably drawn together, meant to be one, recognized by magic itself.

Aconite listened intently as I translated, nodding slowly.

I knew that sense of *rightness*.

I just hadn't known what to call it until now.

But Lorelai was not high fae.

I pushed back from the table.

"I'm returning Aconite to the forest," I told my mother evenly. "As promised."

She gave me a sharp stare, a note of disapproval in the look, but nodded.

Aconite said nothing as I rushed her to her rooms, asking her to pack quickly. She argued that her things would be waiting for her when her time with Gaia was up, that nothing so fine belonged in the wilds of Faerie. Her words dug the knife that had lodged itself between my ribs the moment I woke to Lorelai's note, deeper.

She was right, of course. Faerie wasn't a world of ball gowns and fancy parties. It was wild and free. The sort of place one only needed their knife and a waterskin to survive.

Beneath the trees, I embraced my sister once more. "I love you," I said. "I'll be waiting for the day your remaining years are done. When you can come live with me in Winter."

She smiled and touched my cheek. "I know."

When I turned south, toward the sea, toward Lorelai, there was no hesitation left in me. Only the distance between us.

CHAPTER 32

Lorelai

The forest gave way to humid air on the third day. Neraxis's trail was easy to follow. He wanted it to be.

Trunks thinned as humidity thickened in the air, every step pulling me closer to the sea and farther from the fragile safety I had left behind. By the time the waves came into view, I knew what his presence had been. He hadn't been sent for Firethorn, Aconite or even Mab. He'd been sent for me.

I didn't hesitate.

I dove.

The water wrapped around me like a living thing, power swelling and blooming until my limbs burned with it. Strength returned in a rush so sharp it stole my breath.

My father's guard met me before I reached the deeper currents, steel and tridents glinting in the blue-green light. They closed ranks around me without a word and turned me toward the palace.

Oceanus did not keep me waiting.

The main hall was full. Every courtier, every general, every witness he could summon were in attendance. Neraxis stood among them, expression unreadable. My father loomed at the dais, his presence pressing outward like water against a dam.

"You will answer for your crimes," he said, his voice echoing through the chamber. "You betrayed your kind for the fae. For an alien from another world."

I lifted my chin.

He raised a hand, preparing to pronounce my sentence without waiting to hear if I would defend myself.

"Wait."

The voice was old. Weathered. Unquestionable.

Ephyra swam forward.

She was gnarled with age, her kelpie form etched with the lines of centuries, hair the color of frothing seafoam. Her eyes were sharp despite the years, ancient and knowing. The court stilled in her presence.

"She carries a deity's child. I sense it even now."

Oceanus turned on her, fury blazing. "Then you sense another reason to end this."

Ephyra did not flinch.

She placed a hand against my abdomen.

"You cannot," she said. " Luna has touched this life. It is something new."

A murmur rippled through the hall.

"Something new," he repeated softly, the words like ice. "Something that belongs to no court. That can be claimed by none and controlled by neither." His eyes found mine. "All the more reason—"

"Only Luna may decide who ends her heirs. Either of them," Ephyra said.

Silence fell.

The words rang louder than any shout.

I staggered back a step, breath leaving me in a rush. My hand rose of its own accord, pressing flat against my belly.

And the world tilted beneath me.

CHAPTER 33

Firethorn

The sea was restless when I reached it.

Waves broke hard against the blackened shore, foam hissing across the sand as though the water itself were impatient. I felt her before I saw them.

Oceanus stood at the water's edge.

Lorelai stood beside him, soaked through, her hair plastered to her back, her shoulders held rigid, but she stared at the ground. Two guards flanked her, their presence a reminder of whose territory I was in.

She did not look at me.

Oceanus's gaze met mine with a force that sent alarm bells ringing through me. I searched Lorelai for any signs of injury, but she wouldn't meet my eyes. Another trap? Had I been fooled again?

"So," he said, voice rolling like distant thunder. "You show your face after escaping my prison. You're braver than I thought. Or stupider."

"I came for Lorelai." I ground my teeth, cutting off any further explanation. I owed him nothing.

His mouth puckered. It had been the wrong thing to say.

"What you two have done," Oceanus said, "cannot be undone."

Lorelai's breath caught. My heart pounded wildly. I took a step, but the guards at Lorelai's sides lifted their weapons.

I could burn them. I wanted to. But Lorelai would never forgive me for harming her folk. Even now, I knew that much. Her father hadn't harmed her yet. I fisted my hands at my sides.

His eyes flicked upward, toward the sky lit only by Luna. After three and half days of travel, I'd pushed through the night, desperate to arrive on the sea king's shore, with no real plan for when I arrived.

"I will not spill Luna's blood," he went on.

The words jolted my gaze back to Lorelai. But of course. Luna's granddaughter carried her blood.

Oceanus turned back to Lorelai then, his expression hard, remote. "She has made her choice," he said. "A princess who betrays her court is no princess at all."

His gaze shifted to me. "She is yours now."

Lorelai's fingers trembled at her side, but still she said nothing staring at the ground.

I stepped forward and the guards lowered their weapons as I held a hand out to her. Finally... For the first time since she'd left my bed days ago, she looked at me. She looked at me the way someone looks when they've already accepted a sentence. I couldn't let her give up her life, her birthright, for me.

"Lorelai is not to blame for my escape. She belongs with her court. Will you not show her mercy?"

Her eyes widened, but it wasn't relief or gratitude I saw in them. It was rejection. My gut twisted.

Oceanus growled and spit at my feet. "Your escape?" He leaned toward me, staring up into my eyes. "This is about the creature the two of you created in your haste to sate your whims."

I blinked, his words slow to find purchase. Then, I looked down, at Lorelai's hand pressed protectively over her flat stomach. But... It had been one time. One night.

Warmth swelled in my chest, lighting my veins on fire. Tiny sparks flew from my fingers.

"A child?" My voice was small, the hope cresting inside me, fragile.

Lorelai met my eyes, hers warming and a soft smile broke over her face.

I gathered her in my arms, pulling her close and pressed my nose to her hair, inhaling her sweet scent.

"You're not upset?"

I leaned back, the whole world dissolving into darkness as she searched my face. "I've never been happier."

Her smile widened, the most beautiful thing I'd ever seen. I pulled her close once more, squeezing her to me.

She trembled once before steadying.

Behind us, the tide rolled out. Oceanus spewed venomous words and threats before disappearing into the sea. I ignored it all. All that mattered to me in the world, was wrapped in my arms.

Winter felt quieter when we returned.

Too quiet.

Lorelai slept for nearly a full day, wrapped in a tangle of my blankets. I watched her sleep, finding there was nowhere I'd rather be. When she finally woke, she told me everything. About the seer, Ephyra, and her claim that our child was something new. A creature of both Luna and the Creator's blood.

I listened in stunned silence, my palm pressed flat against her abdomen as though I could feel the truth of it through her skin.

Ours.

Terror and awe braided together in my chest until I could no longer tell them apart.

The next months settled into a rhythm I had never known before. She stole the blankets. Every night, without fail, I would wake to cold feet and her cocooned in every layer within reach, the slight curve of her belly silhouetted against the fire's glow. I started leaving an extra blanket on her side.

She told me a joke on the fourth month. It was terrible. I laughed until my ribs ached and she looked so pleased with herself that I couldn't bring myself to tell her why it didn't quite land.

And I loved her. When the thought finally took shape, it felt inevitable.

"I want to marry her," I told my mother one evening.

Mab studied me for a long moment, her expression unreadable.

"You are the prince," she said at last. "A sea princess cannot rule when I am gone."

"Why not?" I demanded. "She is intelligent. Strong. She's learning your folk's language."

"Our folk," Mab replied coolly. "And you forget, if a sea princess sits the throne, the wards will no longer protect us from Oceanus."

I turned away before my anger could betray me.

Lorelai had begun to tire more easily, the midwife claiming she would give birth in a matter of weeks.

"It's too soon, I'd whispered, after Lorelai was tucked in bed for the night. "Should she not have months remaining?"

The midwife, a fawn I'd grown to respect a great deal these past five months, patted my hand gently. "Your child is not of this world. The deities do not move on our clock."

At night, Lorelai began to moan in her sleep, tossing and turning. I rubbed her back, brought ice to rub across her lips, but nothing helped. I feared what it meant for the two of them, my love and my child. Though it was rare, females sometimes did not survive the birth. I asked my mother, but she was no help.

If Aconite were here, her magic may be what was needed to ensure they both survived.

But there was another I could ask. One who'd yet to show his face since I had arrived on this planet more than fifty years ago. My father.

I sat with Lorelai in the hot springs most of the day, praying to Luna and my father that she would be restored, but each day, the light in her eyes dimmed a little more.

One night, I tucked her into bed and left our room, escaping the palace and disappearing into the snowy dark.

Outside my mother's wards, I whispered her name on the wind: "Gaia?"

I held my breath in the crisp air, awaiting her reply. After all, who better to ask than the one they called mother?

The night was cool, even outside Winter and the wind whipped at my hair. I strained for any sign she was near. "Please, Gaia. If you can hear me, we need you."

The hairs on the back of my neck prickled and I spun around.

Large silver eyes that held their own light glinted in the pitch darkness. My gaze shot up at the sky now glittering only with stars. Luna moved toward me, graceful and lithe. "Firethorn," she said, dipping her chin.

I stared in wonder at the goddess who seemed far brighter, stronger, than she had when we last met. "Luna." I bowed low.

She reached for me, wrapping an iridescent hand around mine when I held it out to her. "Walk with me."

I did and slowly, we turned back toward Winter. "The child will not live."

Her words, said with no inflection, cut straight to my heart. I stumbled to a halt, struggling for air. A million small dreams, futures I'd envisioned, shattered like glass.

"Please," I begged when I found my voice. "Please don't take them from me."

Luna stared with round, alien eyes that held no emotion. "It is the way of deities. There cannot be more than three."

A tear slid down my cheek. "But the child isn't... I'm not..."

Luna's brow softened, and she slid her hand from mine, turning to face me fully. "The creator grows weary. He demands respite. He shall have it."

"I don't understand."

"He will choose his heir and the others must die."

I stopped. "But, the sea king's seer said the child would replace *you*?"

Luna's shoulders slumped, her gaze suddenly weary for such a youthful face. "I am the light that shelters the world. I am the only defense against the dark. I had hoped..." she exhaled a long sigh. "But with one such as Mab, a true name wielder, my work is far from done."

My heart clenched, my hands fisting at my sides. "Why must the others die when one is chosen?"

"There can be only three." She resumed walking and I moved rigidly beside her. My thoughts tumbling over one another in search of a solution.

Luna was silent for a long time, perhaps listening to my tangled frantic mind. When she stirred, my knuckles were white and I bit the inside of my cheek to keep from begging her for an answer that didn't end in the death of my child.

"Mab has learned the power of making bargains with the stars. With such power, she upsets the balance of this world. I was too hasty when I breathed life into your mate and her father."

Mate. The word dug into my bones, wrapped itself tightly around my ribs and squeezed. Lorelai was my mate. The rest of her words struck, sending me staggering backward.

"You want to rid yourself of your *options*." The word she'd used for her offspring, and my father's, came back to me. Now, I understood just how clinical it was. She no longer had need of a backup plan, so she would rid herself of all of them.

She said nothing, letting her silence be confirmation.

"Why can she not take his place?" My voice cracked on the rest of my unspoken words.

"She is not his to claim."

Heat bubbled up in my veins. An anger that tore through me so quickly I couldn't stop the sparks that burst from my fingers. "It's not their fault you changed your mind. You can't take them. Any of them."

Luna's gaze sank to my fingers, to the white sparks fizzling off them. "Your father will choose you, Firethorn. Unless you give him reason to choose otherwise."

CHAPTER 34

Lorelai

I woke alone.

For a moment, I thought nothing of it. Firethorn was often pulled away at all hours. Prince's duties, councils I did not yet understand, and unending list of responsibilities for Mab's heir. The fire beside the bed had burned low, embers glowing softly in the hearth.

I wrapped a fur-lined robe tightly around myself, hands lingering at my belly, round and heavy now, life pressing outward with a weight that felt both miraculous and frightening. The child shifted, and I smiled despite myself.

The fae had their last meal of the night nearing mid-night and I had found them seated at the long dining table that was once the place Firethorn and I met each morning.

The hall fell quiet when I entered.

Not a hush of respect, but the brittle kind, the kind that fractured under scrutiny. Voices dipped. Laughter caught and twisted into something else. I heard my name, half-formed and clumsy in a language I still struggled to grasp.

Then: *Firethorn.*

I looked around the table, searching instinctively for him. Faces turned away. Some hid their smiles behind their hands. Others stared openly, their expressions twisted with disgust.

A sharp pain shot through my stomach as the baby kicked, and I rubbed the sore spot as I slid into an empty seat to rest.

I turned to the female beside me, one I had shared meals with for months now. Her name was Hellebore and she was one of the few fae of this court who was kind to me. Patient as I worked to learn their language.

"Firethorn?" I asked in broken fae. "Where?"

She answered too quickly, words spilling over themselves. I caught fragments. Sounds I knew, meanings I did not.

Then the words that mattered cut through everything else.

Firethorn. Mated. Clematis.

The room darkened at the edges.

No. No. It couldn't be. If it were true, I would feel it in my bones. But there was only silence.

My chair scraped loudly as I stood. Someone laughed. Someone else hissed for silence. I didn't look back as I raced from the room.

The corridors blurred as I searched our room, the ballroom, the galleries overlooking the mountain. No sign of him. No note. No explanation. I wobbled to the window overlooking the gardens that remained in bloom even in this frigid climate. I searched the unending stretch of white beyond them for any sign of his navy coat, of his silver-white hair. Nothing.

A sharp pain seized my lower back.

I gasped, gripping the wall. It was too soon. I wasn't ready.

I staggered toward the hot springs, desperate to draw on my magic, to strengthen me for what I knew would be a difficult birth. Firethorn thought he hid his nervous looks and racing heartbeat. He thought I didn't know how scared he was. The baby was coming too soon. Had grown too fast. And the rapid development had taken its toll on me as well.

Steam curled around me as I slipped into the water, drawing magic greedily into my veins.

I exhaled a slow breath around the next sharp pain that speared my side and tried to bury the hateful words the fae had spewed. It was impossible. We may not be mates the way two fae could be, but my soul yearned for him, my heart beat in time with his as we drifted to sleep each night. Without him, I was half a being. He was made for me as I was made for him.

The pain returned again and again, relentlessly.

I bit back a scream as something inside me shifted.

"You've heard the news."

Mab stood in the doorway.

I surged upright, claws extending instinctively as I called the water. "You're all lying," I said hoarsely. "He loves me and when he returns, he'll set them straight."

Mab's expression didn't change. "And where is he then? If he loves you so much, why isn't he here with you when you need him most?"

Her words were sharper than the pain spearing my middle. I blocked them out, breathing deeply through my nose as the midwife had taught me.

Mab stepped closer, her gaze flicking briefly to my belly. "And if you think his new wife will allow him to keep a bastard child born of a sea-whore, you are mistaken."

I screamed and hurled the water toward her.

Mab opened her mouth, a strange word that failed to take shape in my mind forming on her lips. The water froze midair, shattered, and crashed to the stone floor in a thousand glittering shards.

That was when I understood. The magic my father had always feared. Mab could reshape the world with a single word and I would be powerless to stop her.

I climbed to my feet, wincing as pain ripped through me again.

She made no move to stop me as I skirted around her. Much as I wanted to stop her, to put her in her place, only my child mattered now.

I ran.

CHAPTER 35

Firethorn

Luna's final words circled me the whole way back. *Unless you give him reason to choose otherwise.* I turned it over and over, searching for a solution. By the time the castle came into view, I had found only one.

Lorelai would die.

But the baby had the blood of two deities in her veins.

Even as I thought it, my heart sank. Nothing I did could save my mate. *My mate.* Now that I knew it was true, I wondered how I hadn't guessed sooner. From the moment I'd first lain eyes on her, I'd wanted to remain by her side for the rest of my days.

Now, I couldn't save her, but I could save our child.

"You are finally asking the right question," Luna said.

I narrowed my eyes. "I could end you instead."

She smiled and her spotted ear twitched beside her head. "No."

The anger sparking under my skin was alive and dangerous. "Why not. I have the same blood in my veins. My power is vast."

She turned away from me, trailing a hand over the blades of a fern. As she did, it unfurled, spreading its leaves wide to bask in her glow. Where she walked, flora bloomed and burst with life.

She could hear my thoughts, would know before I could ever act. "Can you all read our thoughts?"

"No," she said without turning. "But it does not matter."

I ground my teeth together. Her cavalier attitude as she discussed Lorelai's end, my sister's, my child's, had fire sparking at my fingertips again.

"Your father will lay down his immortality if you go to him. There is no need to try to end him."

"But then my child will die. And Aconite."

"Yes."

I squeezed my hands into fists, forcing the heat from my veins. I paused. She wouldn't have come down simply to tell me everyone I loved would die.

"Your shortsighted thoughts speak volumes of the infancy of your lifespan. I may be infinite, but even I do not possess the patience for the time it would take you to puzzle this out."

I opened my mouth, but she continued.

"I will make this interesting. If you are prepared to do what is noble, I will make a bargain with you. Your kind are fond of bargains, are you not?"

I closed my mouth.

She turned back, facing me once more.

"Consider this your test, Nephew. Cross beyond this realm to the land of our kind. Find your father. Choose wisely. And I will bind myself to my successor. That heir shall be preserved until such a day arises that Mab is no longer a threat to Peloria."

My father... choose wisely... Peloria... The riddle was maddening and no part of it guaranteed life for both Lorelai and my child. I had no idea what choice I would face when I met my father.

"And if I fail?"

"Then you lose not one love, but three."

My heart sank.

Luna glanced up and I followed her stare. Had I imagined the coldness radiating from above or did the stars this conversation particularly closely?

"Go now, Firethorn. You are right to worry. If you have not found your father before the baby is born, you will lose them all."

Luna lifted her hands and in moments, light burst through the meadow, blinding me as it shot into the sky.

I stumbled against a tree trunk, leaning into it to await the return of my eyesight, my heart rattling down the seconds.

Finally, white halos around my vision dimmed and the world settled into the soft sepia tones of a full moon. In the sky, Luna watched me, her bright stare a relentless reminder of how little time I had.

I reached Winter's castle in less than an hour and slipped into the silent corridor.

I longed to climb into bed with my mate, to wrap her in my arms one last time. To tell her I loved her and our child. But I risked both their lives by even slowing my steps.

I raced past our room, sending my love her way.

As I ran, I continued to puzzle over Luna's words. My father could choose any of the three of us—Aconite, me, or my child. Luna would save only one.

I slid to a stop at the wide yawning cave mouth deep beneath the mountain.

Mab had restored the entrance after Luna brought it down, but I suspected now that Luna had always known she would.

At the entrance to the cave, my skin prickled, magic surging in my veins. I stepped inside, wasting no time on fear or doubt.

In the darkness, I held up my fingers, lighting them to see my way, but stopped after only a few feet. I held my hand high, scanning a solid expanse of ice. Had I been wrong? Was this not the way? I had been so certain.

Sparks warming in my palm, I pressed two glowing hands against the ice and exhaled a slow sigh as it began to melt.

A lifetime later, I paused, letting the fire in my veins cool and stared around the solid wall of ice surrounding me on three sides. My heart drummed against my ribs.

Was I thinking about this the wrong way? A deity wouldn't spend time melting ice.

I closed my eyes, picturing a world of immortals. My father.

Around me, the air buzzed with magic. Not my mother's. Not my fire magic. Something different. I held up my hands, attempting to guide it. It stretched between my fingers, white sparks dancing off my skin, and soft morning light spilled through a tear in the very fabric of this realm.

On the other side, a world of glittering blues came into view. A blast of frigid air hit me, knocking me back a step, but I dug my heels in and stepped through the rip.

The ground beneath my boots was ice, smooth and unbroken in every direction. No sky. No horizon. Light existed here without a source, pale and constant. Only the howling wind and the biting cold let me know I was still alive.

He sat at the center of it.

A throne of ice and rock emerged from the endless tundra, gales of billowing wind whipping at his hair. He, like his throne, was a statue. A mountain as immovable and rigid as stone. He sat, eyes closed, and ice gathered along his shoulders, the tips of his fingers blue and translucent. I glanced at my own blue-tipped fingers, made of flesh and bone where his were ice.

I dropped to my knees.

"Creator."

If he heard, he made no move to respond.

A thunderous crack sounded and my gaze shot to the massive hand gripping the armrest of my father's throne. With infinite slowness, his other hand cracked free, ice falling away. Then, with a speed altogether different, his eyes shot open.

Eyes that glittered like onyx stone narrowed on me.

"Firethorn."

His voice cut through the wind, rattled my thoughts, and I touched my fingers to my ears, finding them streaked in red.

He assessed me coolly, the weight of his stare scraping over me.

"My son."

Power surged between us, vast and inexorable, pressing into me.

"Wait."

He searched my face, disapproval plain.

"Please. You must save my baby... Father."

He raised an icy brow. "You presume to advise me?"

I dropped my head, letting it touch the ground. "No," I breathed. "I beg you."

"This trivial emotion must be cut out before you assume your place here."

"May I speak, Creator?"

I lifted my head, risking his anger.

He watched me, the wind slowing. Finally, he waved a hand, leaning back in his chair as more ice cracked and shattered on the frozen tundra below.

I climbed to my feet, meeting his gaze.

"You once knew affection, connection, with my mother. Would you not care to see her one last time, before you rest?"

He shifted in his seat. "Is Mab well?"

"She speaks of you often."

His gaze unfocused, staring into the distance.

"No. My time among the mortals is at an end." He returned his focus to me. "As is yours."

The fire in my veins died.

"Father. Please," I begged. "Would you not save them both? My mate and my child?"

"No."

The wind howled through the silence that followed, and the cold sank deeper into me than it had since I arrived.

I pressed my forehead to the frozen ground and stayed there.

The weight of his dark stare burned the back of my neck. Then, he sighed. It was a weary sigh. One that spoke of how tired he was.

"There is one rule we immortals must follow. A perfect balance of power requires three. I will not wait for a child to grow into what I require."

I lifted my head. The cold had bitten through my knees, my palms, the tips of my fingers. It didn't matter.

"Choose Aconite."

The wind whipped my back. "You dare—"

"I'm not commanding. I'm asking. She has been raised among your creations. She understands the world you made and its creatures. She will rule them the way they ought to be ruled."

My father arched a thoughtful brow.

"She is wise, and far less emotional than me. Where I would choose my mate, my child, over all others, Aconite has no such attachments. Her heart belongs only to Peloria."

His mouth softened at the mention of his true child's name. His realm.

"You believe Aconite possesses the strength to do what is necessary for my world?"

I nodded.

"And you know what this means?"

I thought of Lorelai's hair spread across my pillow. The weight of her hand in mine. The child I would never hold.

I nodded.

"So be it."

I closed my eyes, picturing Lorelai, imagining a world where she held our child in her arms.

The vision changed.

My baby was cold and alone, caught in a torrent of vicious sea water. Lorelai's gray, lifeless hands released her and she slipped away, sinking to the bottom of a restless sea. I opened my eyes. There was only one thing left to ask.

"Wait."

The Creator rose from his seat, a million icicles cracking and cascading off him. "I have waited long enough."

"Father, I have never asked you for anything. Will you grant your son one request before you end me?"

He paused only a few feet away.

"Seal this realm from the other deities so that Luna will be forced to keep her bargain."

He searched my face, considering. Then he dipped his chin.

"Very well. A deity is nothing without their word. I will grant you this as your final gift."

CHAPTER 36

Lorelai

The sea charged my veins even before I reached it.

I dove from the cliffs without hesitation, terror clawing at my chest as I hit the water hard. Pain ripped through me at once, sharp and blinding, and I screamed into the depths as my body convulsed.

I didn't shift.

I couldn't risk it.

The current seized me and dragged me down, faster than I meant to go, pressure squeezing tight around my ribs as another wave of pain tore through my belly.

Hands caught me before I could sink farther.

Steel flashed and I bared my teeth.

They didn't speak. They didn't slow. They hauled me through the water as another contraction tore through me and I cried out, the sound swallowed by the sea.

We moved fast.

Too fast.

The water around us thickened, resistance pressing in from all sides until suddenly it broke.

I jolted as they dragged me into the bubble of calm water forcing its way through the sea, my body folding over itself as I gritted my teeth against the pain and tried to orient myself to the changing world around me. We were inside a vast sphere of water encased by magic, its walls holding back the vastness of the wild, untamed sea around it.

We were moving.

The bubble surged forward, carried by my father's power, lifting out of the ocean and traveling over earth that had never known the sea.

I barely had time to register it before another spear of pain ripped through me and I screamed, clutching my belly as the guards dragged me to its center.

Oceanus floated before me.

His expression was hard. Focused. Already elsewhere.

"Why did you come here," he demanded.

"I had nowhere else," I gasped. "The child is coming."

"That was a mistake," he said flatly.

Another contraction hit and I sobbed, curling in on myself.

"Where are you taking us," I asked, the words breaking apart. "Where are we going?"

He didn't look at me at first. His hands were raised, fingers flexing as the bubble strained and surged.

"The seer warned me," he said. "Mab's rage is coming."

Outside our bubble, the sky darkened. Heat bled through the air even here, distant but wrong. The edges of our bubble trembled against a great shock that rattled Peloria. I pried my eyes open, trying to make sense of it, of any of it. Our exodus from the sea, the shockwave that rocked the land.

"She believes we have Firethorn," Oceanus continued. "Or she intends to end us all. Including the child. Who can say with that tyrant."

Fear hollowed me out.

The ground beneath the bubble dipped. The sphere descended, water pouring down and out as we settled into a basin carved deep into the land. My father's magic gave, the water flooding out in every direction until it settled into a vast lake. My own magic, fed by the water around us, was diminished somehow, as if such a small body of water feeding my magic somehow made me weaker too. Or perhaps something else drained me from the inside out.

I had no will to focus on it, not when the pain in my stomach threatened to tear me in two.

I screamed as my body seized again, hands clawing at the slick stone beneath me. Someone was shouting. Someone was trying to help. My head shot back, vision dimming at the edges.

Above us, the sky burned.

Fire streaked the sky in bright reds and oranges, darkness closing in behind it.

Mab, I thought distantly as pain surged again and my throat grew raw from screaming,

"Now," someone shouted. "Push."

I did.

The pain broke me open.

I screamed and pushed and the world narrowed to nothing but the tearing and the pressure and the sound of my own voice ripping itself raw.

Then there was a cry.

Small. Sharp. Alive.

I shuddered once, shaking, clutching her to my chest as the lake water lapped around us. Large round black eyes blinked up at me. A whimper escaped me, but I brushed the thought aside. All that mattered now was that my perfect baby was whole and alive. She was warm against my chest. Impossibly, startlingly warm. Nothing like the water, nothing like the cold stone beneath me. I pressed my lips to her forehead.

I stared at her, my heart stretching, expanding until it was so full I thought it would burst, unable to look away.

I had a child.

For one fragile moment, everything else fell away.

Then something inside me drained.

The pull of the sea vanished. The magic that had always lived in my blood receded, leaving me hollow and cold.

I knew what it was even as it happened.

Luna, I thought. It had always been her.

I felt her withdrawal taking with her everything she had given. My arms trembled. Weakened.

I tightened my grip on the child, desperate, but my fingers wouldn't obey.

The world was going quiet at its edges. I had always known it would be Luna in the end—that she would take back what she gave when she had no more use for it. I hadn't known it would feel like this. Like release. Like being finally, mercifully, let go.

My vision blurred.

I looked up.

Oceanus staggered.

His hand flew to his chest. The water around him trembled, his control over it slipping away.

His eyes lifted to the burning sky.

Understanding crossed his face.

The world dimmed.

My arms loosened.

The child slipped from my grasp as darkness closed in.

The End

EPILOGUE

Gaia

The world would come to know the story of Lorelai and Firethorn, not as it was, but as Mab decreed it to be.

They would say the sea was destroyed. They would say Mab called fire from the sky and boiled the waters until nothing living remained. That Oceanus exhausted himself dragging his people to safety. That grief and strain finished what the flames began.

That story would be allowed to stand.

The truth was simpler.

When the door was sealed and the options were stripped away, my sister acted. She did not hesitate when the balance demanded payment.

Luna chose the child.

She withdrew what she had given. Lorelai died first. Oceanus followed moments later, his power unraveling once the last thread was cut.

The stars watched as they always did, greedy for the pain and suffering of life.

Mab's rage struck the sea.

If she had asked me—anyone but the stars—I would have told her what became of her beloved son. But she trusted those cruel glimmering orbs in the sky, even knowing they were her world's undoing.

She believed she had ended her great foe and taken care of the child that threatened her power.

In some ways, she was right. But even had she done nothing that day, Luna would have taken what she gave. My sibling had spent too long among those cruel glittering lights in the sky. They had twisted her mind, and though she sought to best our nephew, in the end, it was he who won.

When I reached the lake, the survivors were already gathering. They did not see me as I slipped into their court, took what did not belong to them, and brought her to live with me until the day she would finally right this wrong.

The child did not cry when I took her. She only looked at me with black eyes that had already seen too much, as though she recognized what I was and decided, in the way of the very young and the very old, that it would have to be enough.

On land and in the sea, they cursed Mab. But slowly, they began to forget the truth. That the stars and realm's deities were the true villains here.

The child slept in my arms, her breathing as steady on land as it had been underwater.

Aconite endured now. Immortal. Peloria's new Creator. It was more important than ever that she did not become what her mother had been.

Firethorn made the only choice left. He severed the path. He trapped us from the source, and in so doing, he weakened us all. His records remained in the tower. The truth of what Mab had bargained, what the stars had taken, what had been buried. Waiting, as truth does, for the one willing to find it.

I could only hope Mab would not grow to be the mighty threat Luna believed her to be.

But Luna would not forget or forgive the bargain Firethorn made.

One day, when Mab's bargains faded and the stars lost interest in their weapon, my sister would be forced to surrender that which she hoarded. She would yield her immortality to the one she named.

Until then, the child must live.

I would raise her.

I would teach her restraint.

I would teach her patience.

I had done it before.

And I would do it again.

The Drowned Fae Realms is coming in 2027

BOOKS BY CASSANDRA ASTON

Prophecies of Angels and Demons

Grave Secrets *– book 1*
Firefly *– Simon's Novella – book 1.5*
Grave Prophecies *– book 2*
Light *– Gabriel's Novella – book 2.5*
Grave Revelations *– book 3*
Parable *– Peter's Novella – book 3.5*
Fated *– Sanura's Kindle Vella*

Deadly Fae Duology

Whispers Among Thorns
Spring *– Book 1.5*

Poison Amidst Blooms
Winter – *Book 2.5*

The Drowned Fae Realms (Deadly Fae Continuation)

Book 1 – *Coming 2027*

Vicious Villains: A Twisted Fairytale Reimagining Anthology Series

Book 1 – *Coming 2026*

THANK YOU

Thank you for reading Winter. If you enjoyed this book, please consider leaving an honest review.

To leave a review on Amazon

To leave a review on Goodreads

Check out everything I'm working on or sign-up up for my newsletter on my website

ACKNOWLEDGMENTS

If you've made it this far, a special thank-you to you. Readers like you are the reason I keep going!

To Brittni and my mom, for being the first people to read my horrible drafts and for reading it again and again as I worked through all the small details.

To Frankie, for sticking with me through another series. I appreciate all you do.

To my content team, for all your support throughout the series and for endlessly shouting about my stories to anyone who will listen.

To my son, who tells everyone he meets about my books, sometimes to my embarrassment. Thank you for being my biggest supporter. The cat is named for you. ;)

To Tivuel for creating such beautiful art for all the characters in the Deadly Fae Series.

To Nicole and Kelly, my editing ninjas. I appreciate all you do to help bring my stories to life.

Thank you.

ABOUT THE AUTHOR

I write dark fantasy and romantic fantasy for readers who want both. Plot that keeps you turning pages at 2 am and romance that ruins you for everyone else.

My books always feature a fierce heroine, emotionally complex characters, and the kind of dark, difficult themes that stay with you long after the last page. But don't worry, no matter how twisted the journey gets, I'll always bring you home to a happy ending at the end of the series. I can't promise the same for novellas.

If you love Ilona Andrews or K.F. Breene, you'll feel right at home.

I write from Houston, Texas, escaping to the mountains whenever I can, fueled by hot chocolate and spite.

www.ingramcontent.com/pod-product-compliance
Lightning Source LLC
LaVergne TN
LVHW050959080826
845145LV00009B/2368